"What would you think if I got married again?"

Annabel couldn't believe her ears. Surely not even Hugh had the nerve to discuss his marriage to another woman when he had just been kissing her so passionately!

"What would I think?" she gasped. Pain and misery swept through her. "I think any marriage of yours would be a disaster, and I pity anyone who'd take you on! You lied and cheated on your first wife, and now you're cheating on your girl friend! Once a cheat, always a cheat!"

"You don't understand—" he cut in.

"Understand? I should think I do! You've got the morals of an alley cat— you proved that with me!" All the bitterness of the past exploded into rage. She slapped him across the face before running from the beach…and from him.

MARY LYONS

caribbean confusion

Harlequin Books

TORONTO • NEW YORK • LONDON
AMSTERDAM • PARIS • SYDNEY • HAMBURG
STOCKHOLM • ATHENS • TOKYO • MILAN

Harlequin Presents first edition March 1984
ISBN 0-373-10673-4

Original hardcover edition published in 1983
by Mills & Boon Limited

Printed in U.S.A.

CHAPTER ONE

ANNABEL felt the warm sensuous Caribbean breeze
wafting through her long blonde hair, as she picked her
way down the steps of the Tristar at Grantly Adams
airport. It was difficult to believe that it was only ten
hours since she had boarded the aeroplane in London,
the time had gone by so quickly. With the other
passengers she walked, stiff-legged from sitting so
long, over to the impressive airport arrival hall.

Although it was only a short walk across the tarmac,
she was relieved to arrive in the cool, air-conditioned
hall. She had expected Barbados to be warm, but the
searing heat of the midday sun surprised her. Eyeing
the lengths of the queues at the four passport control
desks, she chose the one she judged to be the shortest.
There wasn't really much difference, and she could
plainly see that she had a long wait ahead of her.

Thank goodness she had taken Mary's advice and
worn a cool linen trouser suit for the journey! Battling
through the January sleet in London, it had been
impossible to imagine just how hot it could be in the
Caribbean. Mary had been such a tower of strength
during the last two hectic weeks—her friend's job on a
fashion magazine had meant that she had been able to
give Annabel invaluable information on what clothes
to buy and, even more important, where to find them;
it hadn't been an easy task to find bikinis in Oxford
Street during the depth of winter.

It wasn't just the last weeks, Annabel reminded
herself. What would she have done without Mary's
warm, strong friendship during the last two unhappy

years? She shook her head distractedly. Mary was right: she must put such thoughts behind her. Her friend had spoken frankly as they sat in front of the fire in Mary's flat, the evening before her flight.

'You've got a marvellous opportunity to start a new life, Annabel. You're so lucky! I couldn't begin to count the number of people who would give their eye-teeth for the job you've got. A governess, and in Barbados of all heavenly places. Sun, sand and the Caribbean sea—what more could anyone ask?'

'I know, it's a great challenge, and I'm really looking forward to it. Only—well, it's all been a bit of a rush, and I don't know anyone out there . . .'

'Oh, I shouldn't worry about that.' Mary waved away what she regarded as an irrelevance. 'Of course you're going to meet people you don't know, but they'll soon become friends. There's sure to be lots of super men, and with your looks you'll be able to whistle them up two at a time!'

Annabel laughed, but shook her head determinedly. 'Oh no! There's no way I'll ever . . . ever again . . .'

'Oh, come on, Annabel,' Mary interrupted impatiently. 'You aren't going to try and tell me that your life is over? At twenty-four, for heaven's sake!' She paused, and went on in a kinder tone, 'Look, I know life has been tough on you lately. The loss of your parents has been hard to take, but I thought you'd got over Hugh Grey a long time ago?'

'Hugh means nothing to me—nothing at all!' Annabel retorted breathlessly, bowing her head so that the silken weight of her long fair hair hid her face. 'All that was over ages ago. Over. Done with. Finished,' she added emphatically.

Mary sighed, staring at her friend with anxious eyes, not believing a word Annabel said. However, there was nothing to be gained in pressing the point, so she continued in a bracing tone.

'Just remember to look forward, Annabel, it's the only way. What's past is past. Just make sure you leave all gloomy thoughts behind you with the weather!' She rose and went towards the small kitchen. 'I'll make us some more coffee, and you can tell me all about your new job.'

'Well, I really don't have very much information . . .' Annabel had said, and now, as the airport tannoy blaring out undecipherable messages cut into her thoughts, she looked apprehensively about her. She was acutely conscious of the fact that she didn't know who was supposed to meet her, or how they would recognise each other.

The general noise level was amazing. Many of the passengers were shouting out greetings to their friends waiting to meet them on the other side of the barriers, who in their turn shouted back, even louder. The queue slowly inched forward, and Annabel was about to take a step, when her heels were sharply rapped from behind by a small black suitcase. She staggered slightly, and turned in some annoyance to meet the rueful and apologetic smile of the man behind her. He was tall and slim with a smooth head of fair hair. Dressed in light blue slacks, and an open-necked shirt which showed off his deep tan to advantage, he gestured with one of his fine suede shoes to the offending suitcase. Not English, she thought, and his words confirmed her snap judgment, as in a strong, low American voice he said, 'Sorry, honey, I guess I kicked that case just a little too hard!' He gave her a wide, infectious grin, and she found herself smiling back.

'Your first time here?' he asked, as he took in her creamy skin and bright blue eyes, with frank enjoyment.

'Yes,' replied Annabel, turning to pick up her own small travel bag, as the column of people moved forward. 'Yes, it is.'

'English, huh?' he said, and without waiting for a reply he continued, 'Don't worry about this queue—we'll get through eventually. It doesn't matter where you go, it's the name of the game—travelwise!' and he grinned at her again, as he moved up to stand beside her.

'So it's your first visit to Barbados. What's the name of your hotel?' He smiled at her again, accurately reading her mind. 'Yep! I am definitely trying to pick you up, young lady!'

She couldn't help smiling back at the American. 'No hotel, I'm afraid, I'm here to work.'

'Look,' he said, 'why don't we start again, just a little more formal, so to speak. My name is Brett, and I'm here on family business. How's that for openers?'

'Not bad!' she said, enjoying the sparring match. 'My name's Annabel, and I'm here on "family" business—of a sort.'

'Oh boy, you sure are making me work at this! I'm really very respectable, I'd have you know. My mother lives in the south of this island, and she knows everybody! Does she ever!' he added ruefully.

Annabel laughed, and explained, 'It's really very simple. I'm here to teach—well, to be a governess really.'

'Who are you working for? Maybe I know them, and we can really get introduced properly!'

Annabel paused for a moment. She didn't suppose it would matter if she told him, and just in case no one turned up to meet her, he could perhaps direct her to the house of her new employer.

'I'm here to be a governess, to teach the niece of Lord Lister. I understand that he has a sugar plantation somewhere on this island, and ... and that's really all I know,' she added lamely.

Seeing her worried frown, the man hastened to reassure her. 'There's no problem, honey. I can see Helen over there, you'll be well taken care of.'

'Helen? Who's Helen?'

'Helen Ford. She's a real sweetie, you'll love her. Her husband, George, is the estate manager, or whatever, to your Lord Lister. They're a really nice couple, I met them when I was last here.'

Miraculously, the queue had come to an end, and Annabel, her passport returned to her by the smiling black uniformed clerk, walked uncertainly forward.

'Come on, honey,' said her new acquaintance, and he led her through the waiting throng towards a plain, homely-looking woman, dressed in a simple cotton dress and sandals.

'Brett! How lovely to see you again!' said the woman, and turned with a smile to Annabel. 'How do you do? Are you the new governess?' Without a pause for breath, she continued, 'Those stupid employment agency people didn't bother to give us your name, or any details at all. They just cabled, "Governess arriving", and the flight details. Never mind, here you are at last.'

'Look, why don't you two make yourselves acquainted, while I get a porter and claim the bags,' said Brett, disappearing into the press of people around the baggage terminal.

Annabel smiled back at Helen Ford, and introduced herself. Helen explained that her husband George and Lord Lister were busy in the cane fields, and wouldn't be back until late that afternoon.

'And the little girl?' queried Annabel.

'I've left Tasmin with my two children. We have a bungalow on the estate, and since they enjoy each other's company, I thought it might be a good idea for her to stay the night with us. There'll be plenty of time for you to become acquainted with each other tomorrow. I expect you could do with a rest and a good sleep after the flight.'

Annabel was thanking her for making such thoughtful arrangements, when Brett returned, closely followed by a porter wheeling a trolley. 'Come on, let's find your bags, and we can get this show on the road!' he joked, and presently ushered them outside into the strong sunshine.

Helen led the way towards what Annabel recognised from pictures she had seen as a mini-moke. A mini-moke with a difference, she thought, in some amazement. It had a bright white body, no windows except for a windscreen, and over the seats perched on the chassis was a gaily striped red and white canvas canopy, attached to a tubular frame.

'Just like one of those golf trolleys used by millionaires at Palm Springs, isn't it!' said Helen with a smiling glance at Annabel's face. 'You'll find it's the coolest form of transport on the island. Hop in, and I'll just get these cases sorted out.'

They waved goodbye to Brett and set out along the narrow winding road. The lush vegetation on either side puzzled Annabel, who didn't recognise the long, tall green fronds, about six foot tall, waving in the wind. Helen explained that it was the sugar cane for which the island was famous, and on which Barbados's prosperity had been built. The sugar cane market was in a slump at the moment, she explained, and in fact tourism was now the chief source of revenue.

'I'm not surprised!' said Annabel as she leaned back in her seat, letting the cooling breeze waft her long hair out in a stream behind her. 'This sun is wonderful.'

Helen pointed to the left, and turning, Annabel could see the sea, which came nearer and nearer as the road hugged the coast. She gasped with pleasure as she looked at the mile upon mile of pale gold sandy beaches, stretching as far away as the eye could see. She found it difficult to turn her eyes away from such a wonderful sight, but Helen was giving her a potted version of the island's history, and she turned to listen over the noise of the car.

The island had been part of the British Empire since some time in the 1600s, and since 1966 had been a fully independent nation within the Commonwealth. 'We even drive on the same side of the road as they do in England,' Helen pointed out, in an effort to explain just how 'British' Barbados was.

'I hope you won't mind, but I've got some shopping to collect in Bridgetown, on the way home,' she explained, 'and if you aren't too tired and exhausted, it might be a good idea to pick up a driving licence for you at the same time.' Annabel assured her that she was feeling fine, and shortly the countryside gave way to crowded streets thronged with pedestrians that signalled the outskirts of Bridgetown, the capital of Barbados.

I'll never be able to drive through these streets, thought Annabel with considerable trepidation, admiring Helen's dexterous driving skill, weaving down the streets, carefully avoiding the men and women ambling down the middle of the road with cumbersome baskets balanced precariously on their heads.

Leaving the parked car in the care of an attendant, she followed Helen along the crowded pavement. Never in her life had she seen such a spectrum of coloured faces, from the European white of her own skin type, through a multitude of brown shades to the deepest black.

The brilliant colours of the clothes worn by the passers-by and the high-pitched volume of reggae music pouring out of the open shops, left her feeling stunned. Everyone seemed to shout at the top of their voices, and a more cheerful and obviously happy crowd of people would, she thought, be hard to find.

With some relief, she followed Helen into the cool interior of a large department store, and waited beside her while various parcels were collected. She noticed with interest that every time one of the salesgirls gave a customer their change, they always added the words, 'Have a nice day!' and accompanied it with a large beaming smile.

Back in the car Helen explained, 'It's practically a national saying. They really do want you to enjoy yourself; my kids have even got T-shirts with the slogan on.' She drove through yet more winding streets, past the dockside where some large merchant ships were drawn up, unloading their cargoes. 'Now, we'll just call in at the police station and get your temporary driving licence, and then we can be on our way. I expect you're dying for a cool drink!'

By the time they were back on the road again, after leaving the police station, Annabel was feeling hot, tired and thirsty. But as they headed out over the hills on the way to the plantation, the cool sea breeze did much to revive her. She stared, fascinated, at the magnificent scenery and lush vegetation as the car sped along. They had been driving up quite a steep gradient for the last ten minutes, when suddenly they were at the top of the hill, looking down on a coast very different from that she had seen only an hour before. Wild seas pounded on the jagged rocks, and threw large plumes of spray into the air for hundreds of feet. Here there were no long sandy beaches, but a wild, rock-strewn shore that was impressive in its austere grandeur.

'That's the East Coast, and this is where we turn off. Nearly there, it won't be long now.' Helen spun the wheel of the car, to drive through a large stone gateway and down a long wide avenue bordered on either side by tall, reddish-brown trees, whose branches curved over to meet each other. As they travelled down the green tunnel, Helen explained that they were mahogany trees, planted as long ago as the 1700s, and justly famous throughout the island. The tunnel widened, the trees thinned out and there, before Annabel's incredulous eyes, stood one of the most beautiful buildings she had ever seen.

Why, it's—it's an Elizabethan manor house! she thought. What in the world is such a building doing here in Barbados? She shook her head bemusedly, as she got out of the car and followed Helen through the intricately designed wrought-iron arch, flanked on either side by curving red brick walls, and across the broad grey flagstones to the heavy wooden front door. The door, set beneath an arched portico, was thrown open and a very fat West Indian servant, with a wide smile, bade them enter.

The hall was dim and cool after the fierce sunlight outside, and it took Annabel some moments to adjust her eyes to her new surroundings. The hall seemed to be full of people, servants she supposed, since they all wore the same sort of uniform consisting of neat navy-blue dresses with white collars and cuffs for the women, and dark blue trousers and white shirts for the men, their collars being set off by dark blue bow ties. They were all laughing and talking at the top of their voices in what she first thought was some strange tongue. However, she slowly realised that it was English—of a sort—heavily larded with a local patois. As she could only catch about one word in ten, she just smiled as Helen brought up each one in turn, to be introduced. I'll never remember their names, she thought, and realising suddenly just how tired she was, decided wearily to try and sort it out later.

A male servant went ahead with her suitcase, and she followed behind Helen up a great sweeping staircase, along a spacious corridor and through a door, into what was clearly to be her bedroom.

'You do look tired,' said Helen. 'Why don't you have a shower—your bathroom's through there,' she added, opening a door in the corner of the room. 'A shower and a nap will make you feel so much better,' and she moved around the room showing Annabel where to hang her clothes. Moving over to a table set against a wall on which lay a silver tray, ice bucket, thermos jug, bottles of cordials and crystal glasses, she added, 'I should think you could do with a drink! Just help yourself. If there's anything you want, don't hesitate to ring for Josie, your maid. Well, I can't think of anything else for the moment—I'll leave you to rest. I have to see the housekeeper downstairs, but I'll be up in a couple of hours and help you to unpack. You just relax and make yourself comfortable.' She smiled encouragingly at Annabel and left the room.

Annabel looked slowly around the room, quite overwhelmed by what she saw. The walls, from floor to ceiling, were panelled in some sort of pale wood, the panels themselves carved in what she recognised as an Elizabethan 'linenfold' design. And then there was the bed! What a bed, she thought, as she walked across the brilliantly coloured Persian carpet. A genuine, one hundred per cent four-poster bed! Her hands stroked the carved wooden uprights, as her eyes took in the fine pale blue silk curtains which hung at each end. The inside of the curtains were lined with cream shantung and the scalloped canopy was fringed in pale blue and cream.

Still in a daze from the unaccustomed luxury of her new surroundings, Annabel swiftly had a shower and then, aching with tiredness, lay down to rest. Just for a few minutes, she told herself, then I really must unpack . . .

The next thing she knew was that she was being gently shaken back to consciousness, and on opening her eyes saw Helen's smiling face. Helen was apologetic. 'I'm sorry not to be able to let you sleep longer, but Lord Lister will be back soon, and I should get home to prepare my husband's dinner and to see to the children and Tasmin.'

'Of course,' said Annabel, stretching luxuriously against the linen pillows. 'I really shouldn't have dropped off like that, I didn't realise just how tired I was,' and she jumped out of bed and went over to the large window, curtained and festooned with the same blue silk as the bed hangings. Her gurgle of laughter, and the words, 'I don't believe it!' brought Helen over to join her. 'A peacock, of all things!' laughed Annabel. 'This isn't Barbados, I must be back in England!'

'Nasty creatures,' rejoined Helen. 'Everyone is mad about the idea of peacocks strutting on a terrace, but you just wait until they wake you up in the morning, shrieking loud enough to wake the devil. If I had my way, I'd wring their beautiful necks!'

Annabel continued to look out of the open window, drinking in the scene before her. The wide stone-balustraded terrace was covered with purple bougain-villea, winding and weaving its way through the grey pillars; the close-cropped green lawn surrounding a circular fountain, whose spray rose only to fall splattering drops on the water beneath; and either side of the lawn were intricately planted parterres. The neat, small green bushes enclosing beds of brilliant tropical flowers were designed so as to make a complicated but geometrical pattern, and Annabel sighed in wonder, as she reluctantly came away from the window and back into the room.

'Would you like me to help you to unpack?' said Helen. 'I don't have to rush off straight away.'

'That's kind of you, but I'd better do it, then I'll know where everything is,' Annabel replied, as she bent to undo one of the suitcases. 'I would be grateful if you could—well, put me in the picture. It's all been such a rush—I mean, everything has happened so quickly.' Was it really only two weeks ago that this venture had started? Standing in this quiet room, with the late afternoon sunshine pouring through the windows, it seemed light years away.

Annabel strove to explain. 'A fortnight ago, I called at a rather grand employment agency, on the offchance that they might have a job. I wanted to teach abroad, and those sort of vacancies are hard to find.'

Helen sank into an easy chair, and with a sigh of relief kicked off her sandals. 'That's better.' She smiled at Annabel. 'It's the heat—my feet are killing me! Sorry, I interrupted you. Teaching I can understand, but why abroad?'

'Well, I studied French and Italian for my degree, so those languages weren't a problem.' Annabel paused for a moment, and then went on, 'My parents are dead, and . . .' she turned to look out of the window and sighed, 'well, there were other reasons . . .' She collected herself, and turned back to Helen.

'There I was in the agency, having a quiet interview, when this middle-aged woman, Mrs Graham, rushed in. She had to interview a governess immediately, since she was having to catch a train back home to Scotland, to see to her husband who'd had a car accident.'

'We've had a cable from Mrs Graham,' said Helen. 'Apparently her husband isn't too seriously injured. He'll be in hospital for a few weeks, but there's no need for her brother to worry.'

'I'm so glad,' said Annabel. 'You've no idea how confused and upset she was. When the agency staff had calmed her down, it transpired that her brother, Lord Lister, urgently needed a governess for his young niece, Tasmin. I believe there'd been some terrible accident to her parents. A car crash in America . . .?'

'Yes, it was a dreadful tragedy,' Helen sighed. 'Tasmin's mother was Lord Lister's younger sister. He was absolutely shattered when it happened, as you can imagine. He still hasn't fully recovered from the blow.'

'How awful for him,' Annabel said sympathetically.

Helen sighed again, and then in an effort to be more cheerful, continued, 'Well, you'll be a breath of fresh air in the house, and that's all to the good. The only thing I can't understand . . . My dear, I don't mean to be rude,' she smiled at Annabel, 'but you're very young, and really much too good-looking for a governess!'

Annabel laughed ruefully. 'Yes—well, I must admit Mrs Graham had the same qualms. Quite ridiculous, of course! I'm twenty-four and have taught for two years in a primary school.' She shrugged her shoulders. 'I can't help the way I look, can I? Anyway, although Mrs Graham wasn't happy about hiring me, she really didn't have a choice. There was no time for her to interview anyone else. It was just lucky—for me anyway—that I happened to be in the agency at the time, and I . . . well, I leapt at the chance.' She turned appealingly to Helen. 'So you see . . . I don't know the first thing about how or where I'm to teach Tasmin, and absolutely nothing about Lord Lister!'

Helen gave her a sympathetic smile. 'I must say, I think you're very brave to have taken on such an unknown proposition. Right, you get on with the unpacking, and I'll fill you in on the situation here. First of all,' she explained, 'the schoolroom is up on the second floor. It's a lovely room which runs the length of the house, and I know it's stocked with everything you're likely to need, blackboard, chalks, pencils and pens, etc. As to "how" and "when" you teach Tasmin, I imagine that will be something for you and Lord Lister to arrange.'

'Lord Lister . . .?' Annabel looked at her with enquiring eyes, as she adjusted a dress on a hanger.

'Yes . . .' replied Helen slowly. 'Well, how shall I put it—he's not easy if you know what I mean.'

'Not easy? Do you mean difficult to work with?' Annabel's heart sank at the prospect of having to cope with an elderly and irritable employer.

'Oh no!' Helen paused, then said with a rush, 'It's just that he can be very demanding. He's always very polite, of course, but you do get the feeling that if he wants a job done, it must be done immediately! Mind you,' she added, 'George, my husband, thinks the world of him. His Lordship only took over this estate two years ago from his uncle and it was very run down and neglected. He's worked so hard to make it the place it is today. We all admire him enormously for his drive and energy.'

'But what's he like?' asked Annabel, somewhat ashamed of her curiosity, but intrigued to know more about her new employer.

'Well, first of all, he's a widower. I never knew his wife, she died just before he came out here. It's maybe that which makes him so hard and cynical. It's probably very indiscreet of me to say so, but he always strikes me as a deeply unhappy man. Look, Annabel, I think you'd better judge for yourself. I'm sure you'll like him—although what he's going to make of you, I don't know!' she added, rubbing her sore feet again.

'What do you mean?' asked Annabel anxiously.

Helen gazed at the tall lovely girl in front of her. Annabel had finished unpacking, and was standing before her mirror doing up the zip of a simple rose-coloured cotton dress that emphasised her tiny waist and the full swell of her breasts. As she watched her brush out the long ash-blonde hair, Helen said, with a laugh, 'You're not exactly my or anyone's idea of a governess, you know!'

Annabel swung round and with mock seriousness said, 'If anyone else says that to me again, I'll . . . I'll . . .'

'All right!' Helen laughed again, 'but you'll have to face it, Annabel, you're much too pretty!'

'Oh! You and Mrs Graham—it's all so Victorian!' Annabel sighed, as she put down the hairbrush. 'All right,' she continued, 'let's change the subject! Please tell me about this magnificent house.'

'Nobody knows *exactly* when it was built, but probably about 1650. It's called St John's Abbey after the original owner of the plantation, Sir John Strafford. I don't know a great deal about the history of the house before the estate came into Lord Lister's family in the early 1800s; you'll have to ask him for all the finer details.

'One thing should amuse you, though. You must have noticed that huge fireplace over there,' and she gestured towards the magnificently carved mantel-piece, before whose overmantel mirror Annabel had been brushing her hair.

'Yes,' replied Annabel, 'but I don't think I see . . .

Why, of course,' she smiled, 'who would need a fire in a hot climate like this!'

'Exactly! No one's entirely sure, but the story goes that the builder was too frightened to mention to Sir John Strafford that his smart London architect had designed a house for England, and not the Caribbean, and in the owner's absence abroad, went ahead and built them into the new house.'

Helen explained that the estate and grounds amounted to approximately five hundred acres. There were, apparently, only three other plantation houses like St John's Abbey still standing, due in part to the passing of time and the hurricanes.

'Hurricanes?' queried Annabel, startled.

'Well, they're not exactly unknown in this part of the world, but this island has been lucky in that they've mostly passed us by. You must have read about the one that hit St Lucia a year or so ago, for example?'

Annabel nodded, remembering seeing the devastation and human misery portrayed on the television.

'The really bad hurricane, as far as houses on this island are concerned, happened in 1831. Still,' Helen said, putting on her shoes again, 'that was such a long time ago that I don't think we have to worry about it now.'

'Are there really three other houses like this one on the island?' queried Annabel.

'Gracious, no! There's a much smaller version in the south of the island, New Hall it's called—rather small and poky, actually—the other two are in America. In Virginia and Carolina, I think, but I'm not sure. No, this house is unique in this island,' said Helen with a proprietorial air, 'and we're all very proud of it.'

'I'm not surprised,' Annabel agreed, 'it's perfectly lovely.'

'Gracious, is that the time?' and like the White Rabbit, Helen leapt to her feet and examined her watch. 'I must go. It's been lovely meeting you. It's going to be such fun having a friend so near—our bungalow is over there, just beyond that clump of cedar trees,' she pointed out of the window.

'I'm really very grateful, Helen. I was dreadfully nervous about the job, but you've made me feel much better.' Annabel smiled warmly at the older woman.

'I'm glad. I'll have to leave you now. Just go downstairs and make yourself at home. Lord Lister should be in very shortly,' and she left the room with a cheery wave.

With a final glance in the mirror, to make sure she looked neat and tidy, Annabel paused for a moment, wondering what she could do to make herself look older, and more like the 'governess' that people seemed to expect. She tried twisting her hair and placing it on top of her head, but even she could see that it made her look even younger. More like sixteen than twenty-four, she thought with annoyance, and with a shrug let her hair fall again. It was a waste of time trying to alter her appearance. If Lord Lister thought she looked too young, perhaps she would be able to impress him with her qualifications.

Poor old man, she thought, as she went slowly down the sweeping staircase, it must have been hard to lose his wife and then find himself saddled with a young niece to look after. Arriving downstairs, she wandered through the hall, and seeing an open door, looked in cautiously. It was clearly the dining room, the table being already laid for dinner. What a collection of silver and crystal, she thought, admiring the gleaming patina of the long mahogany table.

Continuing her journey of exploration, she passed through a wide entrance, whose double doors were clipped back against the wall, and found herself in a vast room the farther side of which led into yet another large room, which she could see, through the fluted marble columns which divided each area, was an eighteenth-century music room.

She strolled through to investigate further, and was looking with delight at a small harpsichord, when she heard the sound of firm footsteps approaching. Turning, she took a few paces forward, then stopped abruptly, turned to stone like one of the marble pillars—and shocked speechless.

Not so the newcomer. 'My God! What the devil are you doing here?' he demanded.

CHAPTER TWO

SHAKING like a leaf, Annabel clutched the back of the chair in front of her for support and gazed in stupefaction at the man standing in the doorway.

'I asked you what in the hell you think you're doing here?' repeated the man in a hard, angry voice as he walked slowly over to the marble fireplace and stood facing her with his arm resting on the mantelpiece.

She tried to pull her distraught mind together and to say something—anything! Managing to open her mouth at last, she found she couldn't utter any words, just a hoarse croaking sound. She cleared her throat and tried again.

'Hugh . . .!'

'Well?'

'Hugh, I . . . I don't understand. I mean . . .' Her mind was in a chaotic whirl as she tried, unsuccessfully, to make some sort of sense of the situation. Hugh Grey, of all people! And here . . . What was he doing here?

Feeling faint with shock, she momentarily closed her eyes. Perhaps it was all a ghastly nightmare, some terrible figment of her subconscious mind. It just wasn't possible . . . But as she looked again at the tall lounging figure, she knew she was in the midst of an all too true reality.

At last she found her tongue. 'If—if it's any business of yours,' she said in a high, breathless voice she hardly recognised as her own, 'I'm here as governess to Lord Lister's niece.'

'Don't be ridiculous, Annabel!' The man she had

known as Hugh Grey still regarded her sternly, only the rasp of his voice, and the pallor of his face, showed that he too was under a considerable strain.

Striving to collect herself, she clutched the chair more firmly as she endeavoured to bring her chaotic thoughts and emotions under some sort of control. To meet again, so suddenly, the man who had meant so much to her, and from whom she had parted so abruptly and painfully, was almost more than she could cope with.

'I'm not being ridiculous,' she cried in desperation. 'I am the new governess—I am. I really am . . .!' She heard the note of hysteria in her voice, and shook her head distractedly.

'What absolute nonsense!' The man's hard grey eyes regarded the slim girl stonily.

'When Lord Lister comes in, he'll tell you . . .' she protested breathlessly.

Hugh Grey gave a snort of annoyance. 'Don't be more stupid than you can help, Annabel. *I am* Lord Lister.'

'But you—you can't be!' she cried, the full horror of the situation only just beginning to penetrate her mind.

'Well, I can—and I am!' he said, with considerable exasperation in his voice. 'As for your claim to be the new governess . . .' he gave a short bark of derisory laughter, 'I never heard anything so nonsensical in all my life! I'm asking you for the third, and I can assure you the last time, why are you here?'

'But I've just told you. I've told you the truth, I really have . . .'

'I don't know what you hope to achieve by such a ridiculous assertion, but the idea of you being a governess . . . The whole idea is patently absurd!' He regarded her balefully, his jaw clenched, a muscle beating wildly in his temple.

'Now it's you who is being absurd, Hugh,' she retorted with bitterness. 'Do you really think that I would have come within a mile of you if I'd known you were here? Let alone all the way to Barbados,' she added wearily.

'Are you trying to tell me, in all seriousness, that my sister could have so lost her wits that she would engage you—you of all people?'

Annabel gasped with anger. 'How dare you speak to me like that!'

'I'll speak to you any damn way I choose—especially in my own home!' Hugh growled menacingly at the trembling girl.

'For goodness' sake, Hugh—if I'd known who Mrs Graham was, I'd never have taken the job, would I?' Annabel strove desperately to explain. 'You can't seriously imagine that I had any idea who you were? Mrs Graham was in full possession of her senses when I saw her. She engaged me for the position solely on merit, and . . .'

'Merit? What merit?' Hugh snapped harshly. 'You're an art historian—what do you know about teaching children?'

Annabel began to shake with anger and tension. 'Quite a lot, as it happens! I've been working in a primary school for the last two years, and I'll have you know that I'm a very good teacher . . .' She stopped abruptly, appalled to find that she was shouting at him.

'Oh God, what a mess! My sister's really flipped her lid this time!' he ground out the words in disgust. In the pause that followed his bitter statement, Hugh and Annabel regarded each other with consternation.

What am I going to do? Annabel moaned to herself, watching him turn to walk slowly over to one of the large french windows, open on to the terrace beyond.

As he stood deep in thought, looking out over the garden, she examined him closely for the first time. Tall and slim, with black curly hair framing a deeply tanned face, high cheekbones, and wide sensual mouth—he was still the most devastatingly handsome man she had ever known.

He hasn't changed, she thought miserably, as she recognised the old familiar ache in her body. Maybe the past two years had made his face a little more stern, given a more authoritative air to his movements, a more commanding stance to his figure. Nevertheless, he still had an unconscious glitter about him—that sinister stillness and self-control that had always set him apart from everyone else she had ever known.

Her eyes took in the broad shoulders and the slim waist. His sleeves were rolled up above his brown muscular arms, the faded jeans enclosing his hips like a second skin, as he took out a slim gold case from his pocket and lit a cigarette. The strong column of his tanned throat arched as he exhaled the smoke, and she felt again his aura of strong sexual magnetism.

Oh, no! she told herself desperately. Never again! And like a wild animal, she looked around blindly, seeking escape.

Hugh turned slowly, studying her face intently from beneath his heavy eyelids, before walking purposely forward lithe as a panther after prey. She backed away nervously, coming to rest against one of the marble pillars. His hard, cynical eyes beneath their heavy lids held no expression as he paused, gazing at the frightened and trembling girl, before turning away and pulling the bellrope beside the mantelpiece. Within seconds a male servant appeared. 'Two large whiskies immediately—and I mean large,' Hugh commanded.

'Yes, sir.' The servant disappeared quickly, after a brief look at the two tense figures.

Hugh threw himself down into a deep leather chair, drumming his fingers on the arm as he regarded her with a cool, impersonal gaze. Despite his anger at her arrival, he now had himself well under control, she thought bitterly, wishing she could master her feelings so easily.

'It's no use standing there like Joan of Arc about to be burnt at the stake,' he said sardonically. 'Come and sit down, Annabel. We have to decide what to do.' As she hesitated, he spoke more forcefully. 'Do as I say, and sit down. You look as if you could do with a drink, and I certainly need one!'

Annabel moved like a sleepwalker over to a sofa as far away from him as possible, and sat down silently, twisting her hands nervously in her lap. The silence was broken by the return of the servant with their drinks.

'Come on—drink up!' he commanded harshly. 'That's better. Well, I wonder what I should do with you, little Miss Governess? Or should I say Mrs Governess?' he added, lifting a cynical eyebrow.

The drink was helping to calm Annabel's ravaged nerves, and she replied with some asperity. 'It's Miss, of course.'

Hugh—Lord Lister as she must now think of him, she reminded herself—drew deeply on his cigarette, a slight humourless smile twisting his lips, as he studied the beautiful girl in front of him. 'I wouldn't have thought there was any "of course" about you still being single, Annabel,' he drawled.

Flustered, she took another sip of her whisky to steady herself, ashamed to see that her hands were shaking. How could this . . . this disaster be happening to her? All her bright dreams of a new future, all her hopes and aspirations, now lay smashed to pieces—thanks to the despicable man who was regarding her with such arrogant composure.

'Well?'

'Well what . . .?' she snapped, suddenly feeling tired and weary, despite her sleep earlier.

'We were talking about your single state, Annabel. What have you been doing for the past two and a half years?' he drawled, subjecting her to an unwavering scrutiny from beneath his heavily hooded eyes.

'What I've been doing with my life is none of your damn business,' she retorted, flushing under his disturbing gaze. 'Far more to the point is what happened to Hugh Grey? Or was that just a convenient alias, for the purposes of seduction?' she asked sarcastically, emboldened by the strong liquor beginning to flow through her veins.

'Well, well!' he answered unperturbedly, only a muscle tightening along his jaw disclosing the strain that he was under. 'You have become a little viper since we last met, haven't you? How old are you now—twenty-four? Time does seemed to have staled your infinite variety!'

'If, at the age of thirty-two, you're misquoting Shakespeare, it would appear that you've learnt nothing,' she replied furiously.

'*Touché*, Annabel! Very governess-like. I must say I'm enormously impressed that you should still remember my age.' Hugh grinned sardonically at her, as she seethed with a longing to smack his handsome face. 'Hugh Grey, if you're really interested, is still in fact my name. I became Lord Lister on the death of my uncle two years ago. Since he had no children, and my parents were dead, I, as my father's only son, inherited the title and his estates. Satisfied?'

'I couldn't care less,' she muttered, and regretted the childish words the moment she had spoken.

'That's all right, then.' Hugh remained maddeningly calm. 'As for the "seduction" you mention, it would appear that I seem to have a better memory than you. Did I really seduce you, Annabel? I recollect, dimly I must admit, that you were very . . . er . . . very willing, at the time!'

Her face became hot with embarrassment beneath the cynical gleam in his eyes. Trying desperately to preserve what shreds of dignity she still possessed, she lifted her chin and looked him straight in the face. 'At least I didn't pretend to be something I wasn't,' she said scornfully, her eyes flashing with contempt. 'You were married—weren't you?'

Hugh looked at her steadily, his gaze unfathomable as the silence lengthened between them. 'Indeed I was,' he agreed, a grim twist to his mouth, as he rose from his chair and went to stand with his back to her, in front of the fireplace. 'Oh yes, I was married all right.' His voice sounded hard and bleak.

Glancing at the figure before her, Annabel felt the old longing for him twist like a knife in her stomach. The sight of his long, slim body, the broad shoulders topped by the curly black hair, brought back with sharp intensity all the pain and misery she had fought against for so long.

'Why did you never tell me?' she cried out involuntarily. 'Why did you never explain?'

He turned slowly to confront her, his face as hard as granite. 'I'm simply not prepared to discuss the subject. Suffice it to say that there were very good reasons at the time. As to why I didn't explain—my dear Annabel, you weren't around to explain anything to, were you?' he drawled silkily.

'That's not fair! I . . .'

'Your faith in me was amazing,' his tone was heavy with irony. 'Explain? How could I explain anything when you disappeared off the face of the earth?' His hand wasn't quite steady as he lifted his glass to his lips, the glint in his grey eyes betrayed the strain under which he too was labouring.

Annabel saw none of this, as she stared blindly down at the nervous hands gripping her glass, her face on fire. Oh dear, what was she going to do? She obviously couldn't stay on here, not now! But where could she go? Back to England, she supposed... but how?

She did, of course, still have the return half of her ticket in her handbag upstairs, but how could she get to the airport?

Furthermore, she had no idea how many flights there were each week between Barbados and London... As the thoughts chased one another through her mind, Annabel suddenly felt so nervously exhausted that she thought she would disgrace herself and burst into tears at any moment.

Looking down at the dejected girl in front of him, the long curtain of ash-blonde hair hiding her face, Hugh pulled the bellrope once more.

It was answered this time by a majestic figure, clothed in black trousers, an immaculate white shirt and black bow tie. He carried before him a silver tray containing a decanter and some glasses.

'I took the liberty, my lord,' he said in a deep sonorous voice that suited his heavy figure, 'of thinking that you would prefer to have the drinks tray in here.' He set it down on a low table in front of Annabel.

'As usual, Austin, your perception never fails to amaze me. The bush telegraph in this house is running true to form, I see!' Hugh commented wryly.

Austin, with great dignity, ignored Hugh's words, and with a slight bow to Annabel, left the room.

Hugh turned to the girl, still sunk in gloom on the sofa. 'I think another drink is in order, for both of us. Don't you?'

She raised her eyes at his cynical mocking voice, and shakily took the glass from his hands. As their fingers touched, tension like an electric current rippled through her, and she shrank back in her seat, confused and trembling.

'For God's sake! You're quite safe,' he said bitterly. 'Getting a girl drunk isn't exactly my style, you know.'

'I know all about your "style", Hugh! Who better?' She raised her chin at him in an unconscious gesture of defiance, her nerves raw with tension.

'Who indeed . . .' he murmured sardonically, as he allowed his gaze to roam over her figure, an analytical appraisal that left her flushed and indignantly angry. 'Tell me,' he said abruptly, 'it's only idle curiosity, of course, but where did you go when you left London so precipitately?'

'I don't see why I should bother to satisfy your "idle curiosity",' she snapped furiously. How dared he look at her like—like that? 'If you must know, my mother was very ill and I went back home to Northumberland.'

'I see. I hope she got better soon,' he said with cold politeness, his mind quite clearly on other matters.

'No, she didn't. She died soon afterwards,' Annabel said flatly, her anger washing away as she stared down at the glass in her trembling hands. The memory of her mother's last few weeks, as she struggled against terminal cancer, still had the power to wound her immeasurably.

'Poor Bella,' he said softly. 'I'm so sorry.'

Hugh's unconscious use of his old, intimate name for her, together with his kinder tone of voice, brought all her tortured feelings to the surface. Quickly on the defensive, and wishing to wound him as much as she herself had been hurt, she asked, 'And how is your dear wife?'

Hugh froze for a moment, staring at her with bleak eyes. 'My dear wife, after whom you so very kindly enquire, is also dead.' The rasping agony in his voice startled her, and her eyes flew to his face. His mouth was twisted with pain as he ran his hand wearily through his curly black hair.

'It seems as if it all happened so very long ago, and I suppose time really is the great healer that we're all promised it will be.' He shrugged his shoulders resignedly. 'My wife has been dead for two years, Annabel,' he added harshly, his grey eyes as hard as granite. 'I intend that her memory should be allowed to rest in peace. No unkind words such as yours can hurt her now.'

Annabel hung her head in shame. She had completely forgotten having been told that Lord Lister was a widower. In fact she was still having difficulty in realising that Hugh Grey and Lord Lister were one and the same person. What she *did* understand, and the realisation cut through her heart like a knife of cold steel, was that it was after all, *his wife* Hugh had loved all the time, not her at all. The small crumb of comfort, the tiny flame that she had held so secretly in her heart during the past years, flickered and died. She had meant nothing to him, nothing at all!

Not being able to bear the situation a minute longer, she put down her drink and rose trembling to her feet. 'I'll . . . I'll just go and pack my things,' she said in a tight, thin voice. 'Please can you arrange a taxi for me? I expect I can get a flight back to England easily enough.'

'Oh no, you don't!' Hugh's arms flashed out as she tried to walk past him, and swung her around with such force that she found herself pinned up against his hard, firm chest. Startled, she looked up into his hooded grey eyes, staring down at her with grim implacability.

'Just where do you think you're going?' he asked softly, the silky ruthlessness of his voice causing a shudder of fright to run through her figure.

'Let me go! You can't keep me here ...' Breathlessly she tried to break free of his iron grip. Tall as she was, he was much taller, and far stronger, as he ignored her struggles with contemptuous ease.

'My dear Annabel,' he drawled quietly, looking down at her flushed cheeks, her blue eyes bright with unshed tears, and her trembling full lips, 'believe me, you're not going anywhere!'

'I must! I can't stay here. I ...' Her legs began to tremble as she felt the warmth of his body through his thin cotton shirt. Being pressed so tightly against his chest, his face only inches from her own, was so evocative of the past that she began to feel quite faint and dizzy as she stared mesmerised at his wide sensual mouth.

Hugh's strong fingers clasped each arm in a vice, as with a muffled oath he pushed her firmly down into a nearby chair. 'You, my dear girl, apparently came here as governess to my niece. Have you forgotten that—so quickly?' His voice sounded oddly harsh and constrained.

Annabel gazed up into his hard features with dawning horror. *Tasmin!* The whole point of her arrival in Barbados had been to teach a seven-year-old child, newly orphaned and in a strange land, like herself. How could she have forgotten? What must Hugh think of her? Not much, she told herself bitterly, and mentally castigated herself for her selfishness.

Hugh leant casually against the mantelpiece watching the different expressions flit across her face with grim amusement. 'I note that you have, at last, remembered that I have a niece who needs an education. After all the upsets she's been through lately, I think it best she should be taught here for the time being. A new home and a new school would be too much for a small girl to cope with all at once, as I'm sure you'd agree?' he added sternly.

Looking up, Annabel nodded contritely. 'I'm so sorry. I'm really very ashamed. It's just that I've been so . . . so immersed in my own problems . . .'

He cut impatiently across her stumbled apology. 'Be that as it may, you can believe me when I tell you that I certainly don't want you here, and I have severe reservations about your teaching ability.'

She flinched at his cruel words, as he continued, 'However, it seems that, for the time being, I have no choice in the matter. You tell me you're a good teacher,' his voice was heavy with disbelief. 'Well, we'll find out soon enough, won't we?'

I'm in a nightmare—a living nightmare, she thought, desperately casting about in her mind for some solution to her difficulties.

'Make no mistake about my intentions, Annabel,' his voice was hard and implacable. 'Here you are . . . and here you'll stay, until I can arrange a replacement.'

Trembling with shock and exhaustion, she sighed deeply. Hugh was right, the little girl's needs were far more important than any problems she might have. She would just have to remain here, for the present, and make the best of what, with Hugh involved, was likely to be a hard and difficult job.

She straightened up in her chair. 'I'll stay, of course,' she said quietly with as much resolution as she could muster. 'I promise to try and teach Tasmin to the best of my ability.'

'I'm glad you now see where your responsibilities lie.' His voice was hateful in its mocking cynicism, as he calmly lit another cigarette, looking impassively at the girl in front of him.

'However,' she said determinedly, flashing him a glance of acute disdain, 'I'm only staying on one condition.'

'I don't really feel, my dear Annabel, that you're in a position to impose any conditions upon your employment,' Hugh observed dryly, with a mocking grin.

'Oh yes, I damn well am, you—you dreadful man!' she burst out, her feelings of impotent fury and rage gaining the upper hand.

'Tsk, tsk! Not very governess-like!' He smiled lazily at the girl trembling with anger.

'I've had about as much of you as I can stand for one day!' she cried, jumping to her feet. 'I'm only staying because I feel sorry for your niece and want to help her. I insist that you promise to find someone to take over from me as soon as possible . . .'

'Or . . .?' he queried.

'Or I'll walk out out of here this minute, and there's not a thing you can do to stop me!'

'That seems an eminently fair bargain,' agreed Hugh smoothly, his hooded, lazy eyes regarding with amusement the girl who glared at him so defiantly. 'It's an old cliché,' he added blandly, 'but there's no doubt you look magnificent when you're angry, Annabel!'

'Oh . . . go to hell!' she muttered huskily, blushing furiously at the gleam in his eyes, and almost at the end of her tether.

'Alas, I cannot! I'm late for a dinner date as it is,' he drawled, his voice rich with amusement. 'If you'll excuse me, I must dash upstairs and change.' He left the room with quick strides, and she heard him leaping up the stairs, two steps at a time.

She wandered listlessly through the french windows and on to the terrace. The events of the day, and especially the last hour, had left her completely exhausted. She sank down on to a stone bench covered with gaily patterned cushions and gazed, with complete indifference, at the dusk falling over the garden that had thrilled her so much only hours before. The croaking of the frogs and the twinkling fireflies would normally have intrigued her. Tonight, however, deep in misery as she was and feeling more lonely than she could ever remember, these delights failed to touch her.

So sunk in gloomy despondency was she, in fact, that she didn't notice how dark it had become, until with a click the terrace lights were switched on, and she heard Hugh's firm steps approaching. She looked up with a start, and glancing at her wrist, realised with dismay that she had been in a mindless reverie for the last half hour.

She turned to watch him approach. The tailored white dinner jacket, contrasting so sharply with his deeply tanned features, seemed designed to emphasise his broad shoulders and slim hips. Annabel tried hard to look at him with indifference, and only succeeded in thinking how sensationally attractive he was.

'I'm just off,' he said in a bland voice. 'I'm sure you're tired, so I've arranged for your dinner to be served immediately. Austin, the butler, will see to everything. We'll meet tomorrow morning and discuss the arrangements for Tasmin's tuition.'

'Yes . . . thank you,' she murmured dejectedly.

'Don't worry, Annabel. Just have a good sleep, you'll feel better in the morning,' he said softly and kindly, touching her cheek gently with his finger, before turning to stride away.

Later, as she lay in her magnificent bed, looking out through the window at the moonlight shining through the trees, the tears ran down the cheek he had so lightly touched, as she contemplated the ashes of what had, only hours before, been such bright dreams. The exciting new life she had looked forward to so eagerly now held nothing but unhappiness and heartache.

CHAPTER THREE

TOSSING and turning most of the night, Annabel fell at last into a troubled sleep—only to be woken, what seemed minutes later, by a knock and the entry of a slim girl bearing a tray. The young West Indian beamed at her, announcing that her name was Josie and that she was her personal maid.

'This here's a real Barbadian breakfast,' Josie said, putting the tray down on the circular table in the middle of the room. Drawing up a chair to the table, she added, 'Cook say she don't know if yo' want any cooked breakfast, so we just made it fresh fruit and toast. Yo' want any eggs, I can get them—no problem!' she laughed happily.

Looking at the huge chunk of fresh pineapple, toast and marmalade, silver coffee pot and cream jug, Annabel assured the girl that it looked quite enough. 'I never eat a cooked breakfast,' she explained.

'O.K., miz,' Josie beamed at her. 'The mister say he see yo' downstairs in one hour. O.K.?'

'O.K.,' agreed Annabel, smiling at the dark girl, before getting out of bed and going over to lean out of the window. The bright fresh sunlight fell on the garden, which looked even more lovely than it had yesterday. A gentle humming came from behind what seemed to be a hedge of poinsettias. A hedge of poinsettias—surely not? She remembered buying a small plant at great cost last Christmas. The humming grew louder and a cheerful-looking dark man with a wide-brimmed hat, shorts and an old T-shirt moved into sight carrying a hoe. He spotted Annabel hanging out of the window and waved, calling up, 'Have a nice day!'

Despite her depression and lack of sleep, she couldn't help responding to his infectious happy grin, smiling and waving back as she withdrew to eat her breakfast.

Later, leaning back in her chair, with a second cup of coffee before her, Annabel tried to contemplate the future with more equanimity than she had been able to do last night. She had a job to do, she reminded herself grimly, and the sooner she got on with it, the better. Teaching and looking after Tasmin would, she hoped, take up all her time, and although meeting Hugh again had been a tremendous shock, she would just have to cope, somehow.

Her relationship with Hugh was an episode in her life she had fought hard to forget. She'd spent the last two years reproaching herself for being such a blind fool. If the scars of humiliation and disillusionment could still cause her pain . . . She sighed heavily. Well, she'd lived with them long enough already, a few more days wouldn't make much difference.

You mean absolutely nothing to him, and what's more you never did, she firmly reminded herself, remembering with a pang his words of last night. How he's changed, she thought sadly, as she slipped into a pale blue cotton dress. Surely he never used to be so cynical, so hard and ruthless? With an effort she jerked herself back into the present. Thinking about the past was a fruitless exercise, as she knew to her cost. To survive the present would take all the strength she possessed, she told herself resolutely, as she brushed and tied her hair back at the nape of her slim neck.

Quickly checking in the mirror that she looked neat and tidy, so used to her own reflection that she failed to see how young and beautiful she was, she left her room and walked down the corridor.

She slipped down the wide flight of stairs, looking briefly through the rooms, busy with an army of servants, polishing and dusting the antique furniture and marble floors. Directed by Austin, she eventually fround Hugh in the library. Sitting behind a massive mahogany desk, he looked up at her approach, and gestured to her to sit at a chair placed before him, before turning to finish signing some letters.

Sitting amidst the book-lined walls, watching the gentle morning breeze flutter the diaphanous gold curtains at the open windows behind Hugh's desk, Annabel looked at the authoritative figure absorbed in the papers before him, and found all her good resolutions slowly draining away.

Black curly locks of hair, still damp from his morning shower, fell forward across his brow, shielding his eyes and revealing only his high cheekbones and wide firm mouth. Her eyes moved downwards, to where his half-open shirt exposed the dark curly hairs on his chest, the muscled strength of his arms beneath the rolled-up shirt sleeves, the gold pen in his long slim fingers . . .

Annabel's breath caught in her throat, as she recognised the sick excitement flooding through her body. She clutched her trembling hands together tightly in her lap, as she fought to control the sheer naked desire for his touch that flamed within her.

How on earth was she going to be able to go through with this . . . this *arrangement*? It was to be more than flesh and blood could stand—her flesh and blood anyway. Living in such close proximity, and seeing him every day . . . He doesn't even like you, she wailed inwardly; he'd made that very clear last night. It was going to be—it already was—an impossible situation.

Hugh put his papers away, and leaning back in his chair, contemplated the girl before him. Apparently absorbed in her own thoughts, she sat with her head bowed, her smooth hair a shining stream of pale gold. It seemed as if his hawk-like features softened for a moment, but it may have been a trick of the light, as in a strong voice, devoid of any expression, he bade her good morning.

'Good morning, my lord,' she responded, raising her eyes to fix them securely on the window behind him, her face a blank mask.

'There's no need for that . . .' he brushed aside her use of his title with irritation.

'I would prefer that we kept our . . . our relationship firmly within the bounds of employer and employee,' she said quietly, still addressing the window. 'I would also prefer it if . . . if our previous relationship was . . . er . . . not generally known, or talked about.'

Hugh shrugged. 'You can call me what you like, I suppose. The whole business of titles is totally archaic in this day and age anyway. Still, if that's what you want, so be it. However,' he laughed, 'I really have no intention of calling you Miss Wair, so you can forget that straight away! I shall continue to call you Annabel, and you'll have to put up with it!'

Annabel found it impossible to ignore his surprisingly friendly grin, and gave him a faint smile before looking down at her hands again.

'As to your second point—I agree with you. Little would be achieved by raking over for general consumption something which is long dead and buried. Besides which,' he added with cynical amusement, 'I'm not entirely sure that my . . . er . . . girl-friend would be overjoyed!'

Annabel's eyes flew to his face. 'Your girl-friend . . .?' she queried, suddenly feeling quite faint.

'Ah yes, you couldn't have known, could you?' he said blandly, as he leant back in his chair regarding her pale face intently. 'Your arrival yesterday was—how shall I put it?—somewhat *de trop* in the circumstances! I have a feeling that the quiet, even tenor of my life is in danger of being disturbed.'

What about my life? Annabel was still rigid with shock at his news. Gradually, as the silence lengthened between them she brought her inward confusion under control. What did you expect? she told herself bitterly. It was obvious that such an attractive man would have women after him like bees around a honeypot. Just remember that you were obviously only one of a long line of conquests, she reminded herself caustically as she raised her stony eyes to his face.

A faint, humourless smile twisted his lips. 'I've been a widower for some time now, and at my age possibly the word "girl-friend" is too strong. Let us just say that Imogen and I have an . . . er . . . an arrangement.'

'I bet you have!' she snapped trenchantly, and immediately could have bitten her tongue with annoyance at her sharp response.

'I knew you'd understand, Annabel,' Hugh murmured, his eyes gleaming with unconcealed mockery, as she flushed with mortification at having exposed herself so clearly. 'Imogen is a lovely girl, I find her very restful. I'm sure you'll like her.'

'Your private life, my lord, has absolutely nothing to do with me. I'm merely here to teach Tasmin,' she said coldly, the blank mask of her face hiding the turmoil within.

'Quite right,' Hugh agreed smoothly. 'Now, let's discuss Tasmin's tuition.'

Annabel tried to concentrate on what he was saying, as she seethed with anger at Hugh, at herself, and at her predicament. 'A widower for some time' indeed! Marriage had been no bar to his previous activities, as she had found out to her cost. She pitied the poor girl, however 'restful' she was.

He looks tired, she thought with a sudden surprised compassion, as now that his face was plainly visible, she could see the dark shadows beneath his hooded grey eyes, the deep lines of strain around his wide mouth. You can save your pity, she swiftly reminded her weak inner self. It's plainly the result of a night out on the tiles—with the lovely Imogen, no doubt! she tortured herself.

'. . . so you see, the schoolroom should contain all you need, but let me know if you have any further requirements.' Hugh's words cut through the unhappy miasma of her thoughts.

Oh, heavens! she thought in panic. I missed what he was saying at the beginning. With a considerable effort she tried to concentrate on his next words.

'Tasmin has been spending a few days with the Fords. She'll be over in a minute,' he said, glancing at a clock on the wall. 'What I do want to stress is that "lessons" aren't all that important, initially. I'm far more concerned to see that Tasmin settles down here happily. So, if it's a matter of going swimming or planning excursions, that's fine by me.'

He accompanied his words with a warm smile, and Annabel became suddenly breathless and dizzy, as he continued, 'I'm quite happy to leave the timetable in your hands, just make sure that Tasmin's happy.' He rose as they heard footsteps approaching, and a child bounced in through the open french window.

Annabel and Tasmin regarded each other gravely. 'Hello,' said Annabel with a smile. 'I'm your new teacher.'

The child smiled shyly before running over to Hugh

with a wide grin, and gave him a big hug. He picked the little girl up, swinging her around two or three times, until they both stopped, gasping for air, laughing at each other.

My goodness, she's so like Hugh! thought Annabel. The little girl had the same black curly hair and grey eyes as her uncle, who at that moment put Tasmin down and told her to say 'how do you do' to her new teacher. The child did as she was bid, in a light, clear, faintly American accent. Holding Hugh's hand, she smiled at Annabel and said, 'My, you're pretty! Don't you think so, Uncle Hugh?'

There was a pause while Annabel eyed him warily, noticing that his mouth twitched in silent humour. 'Yes, Tasmin,' he said looking down at his niece, 'I agree with you, your governess is indeed very pretty. Now,' he continued blandly, 'why don't you go upstairs with Annabel and show her the schoolroom. I have to go now and see George Ford about a problem with some of our machinery.'

Later, having settled the child down to write a story, 'What I like about Barbados', 'Just to see what you can do, Tasmin. Don't worry about the spelling or your writing, just enjoy yourself,' Annabel settled back and looked at her surroundings.

The schoolroom ran the length of the middle of the house. The sun, pouring in through the latticed windows, made bright patterns on the old wooden floor, which was covered here and there with gaily coloured, locally woven rugs. The sun also dusted the child's dark curls, studiously bent over her book, as sucking her pencil every now and then, she laboriously wrote her story. The time passed swiftly and both Annabel and Tasmin were surprised by Josie's arrival with cool orange juice and biscuits.

'I'se hoping yo' working real hard fo' yo' teacher,'

Josie warned Tasmin, in mock seriousness, ''cos Hannah's goin' to be real mad if yo' ain't!'

Hannah, it appeared, had been seconded as a temporary nanny on Tasmin's arrival at the plantation; and despite seven children of her own, had gathered the lonely little girl to her ample bosom. She took her duties seriously, and had a strong maternal interest in all Tasmin's doings.

'You can tell Hannah that she's doing very well indeed,' said Annabel, having read the piece Tasmin had just written, gaining a grateful smile from her new pupil. 'Now,' she continued, 'I think we've done enough for the moment. How about showing me around the garden, Tasmin?'

They spent the rest of the morning walking hand in hand around the grounds. It really was a hedge of poinsettias that Annabel had seen that morning. She marvelled at the lush, tropical plants that seemed to grow so easily in the rich soil and sunny climate. Tasmin led her through a wrought-iron gate set in a high hedge, and they found themselves in a swimming-pool enclosure.

'This used to be a rose garden,' said Tasmin, playing hopscotch on the grey tiles which surrounded the shining blue water. 'Uncle said he had enough flowers, and turned it into a pool. It's nice, isn't it, but I much prefer the beach. Can we go there some time soon?'

'Of course we can,' said Annabel, looking around her. What a heavenly place, she thought, almost like a secret garden. Her eyes took in the raised flower beds set back aganist the dark leaves of the hedge, the small gothic-turreted changing rooms either side of what appeared to be a poolside bar. She could have spent much longer enjoying the tranquil surroundings, but Tasmin was far more interested in showing her the old outbuildings, once so important to the life of the plantation, and now no longer in use.

The old windmill was still standing, although it looked rather the worse for wear. Tasmin was a mine of information, having spent most of her holidays with her parents at St John's Abbey.

She explained that the windmill had been used to crush the sugar cane until about the 1880s, when the now disused syrup factory had been built. 'Just fancy,' she said, 'Uncle said the old factory was still being used after the war.'

'Just fancy!' murmured Annabel, looking at the ruined buildings in some disbelief. The windmill had stood the test of time far better than the more recently built 'factory'.

They continued their tour of inspections, past the old cow byres and across a croquet lawn in front of the house, to stand looking at the fields of cane, waving in the breeze. The green fields seemed to stretch forever, as Tasmin explained what a hard, difficult job it was to cut the cane. 'Uncle has some big machines to do it, but he says it isn't nearly as good as when there were enough men available to cut it by hand.'

The old bathhouse, thirty yards from the main building, made Annabel smile. It contained three large Victorian hip-baths in perfect condition, together with other important bathing items of the time, such as huge china jugs for filling the baths, and mahogany towel stands. 'It sure must have been a big deal to have a bath in those days,' said Tasmin, climbing into one of the baths. 'The visitors really love coming in here.'

'Do you have many visitors?' asked Annabel idly, and was surprised when Tasmin explained that every other Sunday the house, downstairs only, and grounds were open to the public, the proceeds going to charity.

'It's a frightful drag, really—but one has to do one's bit,' said the child in a wickedly accurate imitation of Hugh's upper-class drawl.

Annabel's lips twitched as she tried to control her amusement. 'Tasmin! That's not at all polite,' she remonstrated.

'Oh really? Don't you think so . . .? I'm frightfully sorry—do forgive me!' replied a grinning Tasmin, using the same tones as before.

Annabel sank down on an old horse mounting block outside the bathhouse, and roared with laughter. 'Oh dear! I really shouldn't encourage you, it's very wrong to imitate your elders,' she said, wiping away the tears of mirth.

'Absolutely shocking conduct!' continued Tasmin, in the same vein. 'Quite . . . quite dis-disgraceful in one so young. Do excuse me . . .'

Hugh, suddenly coming around the side of the house at that moment, found them with their arms around each other, hysterical with laughter.

'Do excuse me . . .' he began, and frowned as they both started giggling again. Annabel pulled herself together, and with a warning squeeze on Tasmin's hand, gave Hugh her full attention, the child still shaking with suppressed mirth.

'You didn't take the keys,' he said abruptly, putting a small bunch into Annabel's hands.

'The keys?' she said in some confusion.

'For the mini-moke, of course. I told you all about it. Don't you remember?'

'Oh yes . . . yes, of course,' she lied. Heavens, she thought, that must have been what he was talking about this morning . . .

That will teach you to concentrate, my girl, she admonished herself as she and Tasmin followed him to the garage block. He opened the door and pointed to a vehicle, exactly the same as the one in which she had been driven from the airport, except that instead of red and white, it had a blue and white striped canopy.

'You and Tasmin will be able to come and go as you like,' he explained. She stuttered her thanks, but he brushed them aside as a matter of no consequence, and strode off back into the house.

Annabel's eyes followed his departing figure with considerable perplexity. It was really very kind of him to ensure that she had a means of transport around the island, and it was patently obvious that he adored Tasmin. On the other hand, he could be so cruel and stern—like yesterday, she remembered with a shudder. She shook her head and sighed with confusion, as they continued their tour.

Over lunch in the schoolroom, served by the ever-cheerful Josie, they decided to go down to the sea in the afternoon.

They found the beach eventually after Annabel, following Tasmin's erratic directions, had lost her way a few times. Situated in a private cove owned by Hugh, as well as waving palms and silky, soft sand, the beach possessed a large changing hut with a shower attached. What a magical place, she thought, grateful that there was no one else about to see her pale white skin, as she climbed into a minimal black bikini.

Later, keeping a careful eye on Tasmin playing in the surf, she stretched out under the shade of a palm tree, sighing with pleasure. For an hour or so she would endeavour to try and forget Hugh, and the desperately unenviable and unhappy position in which she now found herself. For the moment it was enough just to soak up the warmth of the sun's rays, and be grateful to have escaped from the cold damp British winter.

The peace and quiet of the following three days did much to soothe Annabel's disturbed and painful emotions. Hugh had been hardly in evidence, almost as if he was deliberately avoiding her company, she thought bitterly. However, the enjoyment of Tasmin's quaint grown-up conversation, and the delight any teacher would feel, faced with an intelligent child who soaked up everything Annabel could teach her, helped immeasurably. Plus, of course, the wonderful golden sand and the breathtaking blue sea. It had all combined to pour balm on her troubled spirits.

After saying goodnight to Tasmin, who liked to talk about her parents and their life together before going to sleep, Annabel would retire to her own room. There, after a long soak in the bath, she would sit down to a supper brought up by Josie. After the first terrible evening, when she had to eat alone in the huge dining room, she had informed Austin quite firmly that henceforth she would have her evening meal in her room. Her request had been acceded to, with a bow and a smile.

Each evening, as she sat by her open window, glancing through some of the books she had found in the library, she had heard Hugh's sports car roar off into the night. Being a light sleeper, she had also heard his return in the not so early hours of the morning. He looked more tired and haggardly handsome each succeeding day, but on their occasional meetings around the house and grounds, Annabel didn't feel encouraged to speak to him, let alone comment on his tired appearance. His manner was curt and dismissive, and he was seemingly preoccupied with problems which obviously didn't concern her.

On the fourth morning following her arrival, Annabel and Tasmin went into Bridgetown with Helen Ford. It was an uneventful sightseeing trip,

apart from Annabel managing in the nick of time to
prevent Tasmin from buying a T-shirt with the
inscription 'Hello Sailor—I feel gay today' and having
to refuse the child's request for a trip on the *Jolly
Roger*. The ship, a life-size replica of an Elizabethan
galleon, looked great fun with its vivid red sails and
crew dressed as pirates. However, close inspection had
shown Annabel that a trip out to sea would be fraught
with difficulties. As the returning passengers trooped
down the gangplank, it was obvious that wine, women
and song were the order of the day. She managed to
snatch Tasmin out of the way of a man swaying
around happily with a bottle clutched in his hand, and
quickly suggested that they retrace their steps to a café
where they had arranged to meet Helen.

'Sorry, darling,' she said, smiling at the little girl.
'It's not suitable, really it isn't.'

'Because some of the people have been drinking?'
asked Tasmin, a worldly-wise look sitting oddly on
her young face.

'Er . . . yes. Your uncle really wouldn't approve.'

'No, he wouldn't,' laughed Tasmin. 'What an awful
shower!' she added, mimicking Hugh's voice.

'Now, Tasmin!' Annabel tried not to laugh. 'I've
told you not to do that any more. You know your
uncle would be furious if he found out.'

'O.K., but only because *you* ask me not to. I do love
you being here, Annabel,' Tasmin added shyly.

'Well, I love being here with you,' she responded,
touched by the child's need of love and affection. She
gave the little girl a big hug and kiss before entering
the café to join Helen in a cool drink.

The rest of the day passed quietly enough. They
lunched in the schoolroom and then both went to their
respective rooms; Tasmin to have a short sleep, and
Annabel to write a letter to her friend Mary. She was

careful not to disclose that Lord Lister was Hugh Grey, and concentrated on describing the delightful scenery and wonderful climate.

'Now,' said Annabel in the mid-afternoon, 'we are going to have a history lesson. Come along,' she took Tasmin's hand and led her downstairs into the empty drawing room, where heavy oil paintings gleamed on the white walls. She directed Tasmin's attention to a large picture of the Battle of Trafalgar. 'I saw this the other day, and I thought I'd tell you about Lord Nelson. You'd better concentrate,' she warned the little girl with a laugh, 'because I'm going to give you a test tomorrow morning, to see how much you've managed to remember!'

With quick intelligence Tasmin assimilated most of the facts of her lesson with ease, and when Annabel had finished, the child wandered into the adjoining music room.

'I think these are much more interesting. They're real people, or they were,' the little girl said, pointing to a line of family portraits which looked down from the walls.

'All right, it's your turn to give me a lesson—on the family history,' Annabel smiled, listening idly as Tasmin outlined the brief lives of the various men and women gracing the room.

'This one, of wicked Henry Lister, is my absolute favourite.' The child pointed to a large oil painting of an eighteenth century man, leaning nonchalantly against a stone pillar covered in ivy. 'Doesn't he look like Uncle Hugh?'

Doesn't he just! thought Annabel, staring wide-eyed with shock at the slim, casually lounging figure, gazing out at the world with cynical grey eyes. The man's black hair curled carelessly about his dynamically masculine features, his mouth curved into a sardonic smile remarkable for its expression of cruel dissipation.

'He came to a bad end,' Tasmin explained. 'But he is like Uncle Hugh, isn't he?'

'Oh yes,' Annabel replied, still bemused at the close resemblance between the two men, despite the intervening two hundred years. 'Oh yes, the very picture of a debauched libertine!' she added slowly, unconscious of the child's wide-eyed interest.

She shook her head distractedly, and looked at her watch. 'It's time for you to have some milk and biscuits. Run along now, and we'll then go for a swim in the pool.'

Left alone, she moved slowly around the room, sinking down almost without thought on to a music-stool. The quiet stillness of the room surrounded her slim figure as she gazed mesmerised at the portrait of wicked Lord Lister. Everything about the portrait, the facial resemblance, and the cynical grey eyes, even the casual stance, served to remind her of the first time she had met Hugh.

Annabel moved restlessly on the stool as the unwanted memories came stealing insidiously back into her mind. She had been such an innocent ... when they had first met. Looking back now, she could hardly recognise the gullible young girl she had once been.

She hadn't been sure what she wanted to do after leaving university. She had found herself, twenty-one years of age, fluent in French and Italian—and still a virgin! Her friends had laughed at her, but she hadn't minded. Of course, she'd had boy-friends at college, but since they had meant very little to her, she had remained cool and untouched by the passions that had swamped some of her friends. Until, that was, she went to London, to work behind the scenes of the large London fine art auction house, known as 'The House' to those who worked there. She had been incredibly lucky to get the highly coveted job. The head of her department, Mr Oakes, was one of the world's acknowledged experts on early Italian Renaissance paintings, and a hard taskmaster. Her fellow workers had regaled her, during her first months, with lurid tales of past assistants who had fallen foul of her boss.

Although she had been a very small cog in the wheel of his department, her obvious delight in the art of the period, and her instinctive 'feel' for a good painting—or a great one—among the thousands that passed through the department, kindled his interest in the newcomer. Finding her receptive, he had widened her knowledge immeasurably. When clients called with pictures for valuation or sale, he would take her with him to the front desk in the grand foyer, where he discussed the paintings with the clients and assessed their possible auction value.

Annabel had been called downstairs one warm spring day, to find Mr Oakes talking to a tall, slim man with dark curly hair, who turned at her approach looking at her intently out of cool grey eyes.

'Annabel,' said Mr Oakes, 'this is Hugh Grey, who's brought us this picture for disposal,' and he turned away to examine the landscape painting more closely.

'Actually, strictly speaking it's not my picture,' explained Mr Grey in a strong, firm voice, as he leant casually against the desk. 'It belongs to my aunt, who wishes to dispose of it.'

Annabel had stood still as a statue, frozen rigid with shock. She had never seen such a devastatingly handsome man in her whole life! Feeling suddenly breathless and lightheaded under his penetrating gaze, she had thought that he must be the living embodiment of every girl's dream of a Byronic hero.

Trying to collect her whirring emotions, and feeling dazed and slightly sick, she forced herself to turn away and concentrate on what Mr Oakes was saying. She could feel the stranger's eyes boring into her back, and was absurdly thankful that she was wearing one of her prettiest dresses.

You're behaving like a stupid teenager, she had reproved herself sternly, turning confidently to face Mr Grey, only to be cast into confusion once more, as she met his full gaze. He can read my mind, she thought with panic, as his eyes ranged slowly over her face and figure, and what's more, he's . . . he's mentally undressing me! She had blushed a deep crimson, made a hurried excuse to the surprised Mr Oakes, and escaped upstairs.

Leaving work that evening, she had been striding blithely down Bond Street, when her arm had been caught firmly from behind and she had been spun round to face Mr Grey!

'What are you doing?' she had gasped nervously. 'What—what do you want?'

'What do I want? You, of course! As for what I'm doing—I'm going to take you out to dinner.'

Masterfully ignoring her protests, he had bundled her into his Jaguar. With extreme reluctance he had agreed to take her back to her small flat to change, pacing restlessly up and down the street outside, while she feverishly hunted through her clothes for something suitable to wear.

On her reappearance with flushed cheeks and wearing her best dress, he had impatiently issued her into the car before driving swiftly through London to a small riverside restaurant. There, as they looked out over the Thames, he had ordered a meal, and demanded that she tell him her life story.

Annabel could never remember what she had eaten that night. All she could recollect was that they had talked incessantly, so immersed in their absorption with one another that when they looked up, it was to find all the other diners had left.

Hugh had driven her home, gently helping her out of the car and escorting her to the front door, where he had taken her hand and raised it lightly to his lips. 'I'm not going to let you go—not now I've found you at last,' he had said gravely, before running swiftly back down the steps and roaring off into the night.

That had been the start of their romance, a romance that had totally and dramatically changed her life. As the cold harsh days of blustery spring gave way to the warm hazy days of summer, Annabel realised that for the first, last and only time in her life, she was in love.

That Hugh, so handsome, so much older and more experienced, should love her as she loved him seemed almost a miracle beyond belief. And yet, as he monopolised every free moment of her time, pursuing her with ruthless determination, she slowly came to accept and believe his avowed love and devotion.

Annabel shivered nervously, the sound of approaching footsteps bringing her sharply back to reality, as she stared with contempt at the painting in front of her. It was obvious that Hugh was a carbon copy of the dissipated eighteenth-century figure. If she hadn't been such a silly stupid fool, so much in love as to be totally incapable of rational judgment, she would have realised that Hugh Grey was a charming philanderer, as indeed he had proved to be.

Her unhappy thoughts were interrupted by the entrance of Tasmin, anxious to go swimming in the pool. With firm determination, Annabel shook off her sad recollections and went upstairs to fetch her bikini and towel.

Tasmin, who could swim like a fish, was keen to practise her diving. 'Watch me, Annabel, watch!' she called, as she toppled forward once more into the pool.

'Much better,' said Annabel with a laugh, as the little girl surfaced beside her in the water, 'but you must remember to keep your legs straight. You looked just like a spider!' she grinned, giving Tasmin, who was hanging on to her in the deep end, a kiss of encouragement. 'Off you go and try again.'

'I'm glad to see you're both keeping cool,' a dry lazy voice said from behind her shoulder, and spinning around in the water, Annabel gazed up into Hugh's smiling face.

'Oh ... er ... yes,' she said confusedly, as she looked at the tall, lithe figure poised on the edge of the swimming pool. His broad-shouldered, tanned body was clothed only in a slim pair of dark bathing trunks, and she found it difficult to tear her eyes away from the taut firm muscled thighs of his long brown legs.

She blushed furiously as she caught his look of lazy amusement, and dived beneath the water to cool her body, which had suddenly become unaccountably hot and feverish. When she surfaced, it was to find Hugh giving Tasmin some lessons in how to hold her arms when diving, before going to the board at the end of the pool to show her how it was done.

He looks magnificent, she thought despairingly, the old familiar ache gripping the pit of her stomach as she watched him pass her in a fast crawl on his way down the pool. The sooner she left the water and his disturbing presence the better, she decided, swimming slowly down towards the shallow end where Hugh and Tasmin were talking together.

Standing waist-high in the water, Annabel was about to mount the wide steps of the pool when

Tasmin turned to her excitedly. 'I've just been telling Uncle about the *Jolly Roger*, and he agreed it wasn't suitable for me at all!' she laughed.

'Annabel was quite right,' he said, throwing an amused grin in her direction.

'. . . and then we had lunch,' Tasmin was obviously going through her day with Hugh, 'and then we had a history lesson. I know all about Lord Nelson now, and the Battle of Trafalgar. It was so sad that poor old Nelson was killed. Annabel pointed out his ship in the picture in the drawing room.'

'It would seem that your governess is proving to be a better teacher than I'd realised,' he said, smiling wryly at Annabel, who acknowledged his compliment with a small, distant nod of her head, as she prepared to leave the water.

'. . . and then,' Tasmin splashed water at Hugh, 'I gave her a lesson on our family pictures. I was very good and remembered all the family history very well,' she said smugly. 'Annabel liked the one of poor Henry Lister, who came to a bad end. She agreed it looked just like you. The "very picture of a debauched libertine",' Tasmin said happily, mimicking Annabel's cold English voice.

There was a long silence as Annabel stood frozen, watching the smile fade from Hugh's face. She felt as if she had been turned to stone, as she watched him stiffen, and his features assume an expression of grim, implacable anger.

Tasmin, quickly realising that she had said something wrong, put her hand over her mouth looking at Hugh and Annabel with anxious eyes.

'I think it's time for you to go and have your supper,' Hugh said blandly to Tasmin. 'Run along now. I just want to have a brief word with Annabel.'

Annabel stood trembling in the water as she watched the subdued little girl close the wrought iron gate behind her. Shutting her eyes, she waited for Hugh's wrath to descend on her head.

CHAPTER FOUR

'I'M afraid I don't find your remarks about me very amusing, Annabel,' Hugh purred with menace from behind her shoulder, as he swiftly turned her trembling figure to face his hard, angry eyes.

'I—I'm sorry. I didn't know Tasmin was listening to me. I—I just ... I was just thinking aloud ...' she murmured unhappily, her head bowed, unable to look at his face.

Hugh gave a dry bark of sardonic laughter. 'I hardly think that qualifies as an excuse, do you?'

Annabel shook her head distractedly, unable to answer him, acutely conscious of his long slim fingers grasping the top of her arms, and the close proximity of his body.

'In future, my dear girl,' he drawled silkily, as he put a hand under her chin, lifting her face to his, 'you will keep any thoughts you might have about my—my proclivities entirely to yourself.'

Annabel stood quivering before him, imprisoned like a fly in amber by the deep gleam in his hooded grey eyes. Her heart was beating rapidly, and she found it difficult to breathe.

As he looked down at the beautiful girl's large blue eyes, flushed cheeks and trembling soft lips, Hugh's harsh features underwent a subtle change as he relaxed his hold of her chin and slowly ran his hand down her slim neck, to brush with light fingers the swell of her full breasts exposed by the scanty bikini.

Jerking back as if she had been stung, Annabel blushed a deep crimson beneath his unwavering stare.

59

'Is my touch so distasteful to you, Bella?' he asked quietly, sliding an arm about her waist, as he continued to gently stroke her soft skin.

'You . . . you know it is,' she whispered, trembling violently from the touch of his fingers, but unable to move away, paralysed by the tentacles of sexual tension which coiled about them.

'Then the method by which to punish you for your unkind remarks about me is clear,' he said thickly, putting both his arms about her and clasping her slim body firmly against his bare chest.

'Oh no!' she cried, as she saw his clouded grey eyes suddenly flash with passionate desire. 'No . . . please!' she begged, as, with deadly intent, his dark head came down towards her.

His mouth possessed hers, firmly and inexorably, in a kiss of scorching intensity, crushing her lips so fiercely that the relentless pressure forced them apart. Her muffled protest became an inaudible moan, as he began an exploration of the inner softness of her mouth that was a lustful invasion of her shattered senses.

Annabel struggled as best she could, but she was powerless against his superior strength as he contemptuously ignored her hands beating desperately against his chest; her futile kicks against his legs being baffled by the water in which they were both standing. It was only when she was so exhausted that she could struggle no more that he released the hateful pressure and removed his mouth, to stand looking down at her with unfathomable eyes.

'You're . . . you're despicable!' she gasped, raising a hand to her bruised lips and glaring at him with large blue eyes awash with tears.

'That was merely to teach you a lesson,' he said grimly, 'a lesson which I hope you will heed. Kindly, in future, keep your thoughts about me strictly to yourself.'

'When I called you a debauched libertine,' she cried in fury, 'I was absolutely right! That's exactly what you are, and . . . and I'll scream it from the rooftops if I want to! Especially at the airport when I leave tomorrow,' she added, shaking with rage.

'Really?' said Hugh, his eyes gleaming with mockery.

'Really!' she retorted loudly, turning to walk up the shallow steps out of the pool.

She had only taken one step when she felt her hair, tied in a ponytail, jerked sharply. Suddenly she was flat on her back, being towed up the pool by Hugh, who came to rest with his feet touching the bottom, while she found herself completely out of her depth— literally and figuratively.

Her cries of anguish availed her nothing, as he crushed her ruthlessly in his arms, looking down at her helplessly struggling figure.

'You aren't going to the airport tomorrow,' he said quietly, with infinite menace. 'You promised to stay here and teach Tasmin, and I'm holding you to that promise. Is your word so lightly given, Annabel?'

'I can't . . . I can't stay here. You must see that . . .?' she protested, totally exhausted by the determined fight she had put up against his earlier assault.

'You gave me your word that you'd stay here until I could find a replacement. Are you intending to go back on your promise?' His face was stern and hard, only his eyes seemed to soften and gleam as he gazed down at the distraught girl.

'I . . .' she looked around her desperately for some means of escape. His expression might look as if it was carved from granite, but although one hand was holding her so firmly, the other was beginning to gently stroke the soft skin of her waist.

'Let me go! You must let me go . . .!' she pleaded.

'Not until I have your solemn promise that you will stop threatening to leave. Tasmin needs you, surely you can see that?'

Annabel gasped as his hand came slowly up to clasp her breast. 'Yes, yes . . . I . . . I p-promise,' she stuttered, trying to twist away from his grip.

'Good girl,' he murmured. She sagged with relief and her heart stopped racing, as he removed his hand from her breast. Alas for her piece of mind, he did not let her go but brought his hand up to gently stroke her cheek, while still clasping her firmly against the curly hair of his chest.

'You said . . . you said you'd let me go!' she cried, as his head descended towards her once again, his lips softly kissing the outline of her mouth, a touch both gentle and insistent. She gasped, her lips parting of their own volition, as her treacherous body responded to the possession of his mouth, melting with desire in his arms.

His kiss seemed to last for ever, as she floated mindlessly in the water. Hugh removed his mouth at last, looking down at the dazed girl. 'There's no need to look so shattered, Annabel,' he drawled softly. 'It was only a kiss!'

'I—I hate you!' she gasped, breaking free of his arms and swimming shakily away to the end of the pool.

'Oh yes?' Hugh laughed wryly, following her in a lazy crawl.

'I said you were despicable—and so you are!' she cried, seizing up her towel and running over to the gate set in the high green hedge. 'Your behaviour is absolutely . . . absolutely revolting! What about your girl-friend?'

'We'll leave Imogen out of this, if you don't mind,'

he said coldly, walking over to one of the changing huts.

'It wouldn't do you any harm to recall her to mind—*my lord*—even if you used to have difficulty remembering you were a married man!' she shouted viciously banging the gate behind her retreating figure.

Sitting on the beach the next morning, letting the soft sand trickle through her fingers, Annabel shuddered at the recollection of her encounter yesterday with Hugh. She had spent a sleepless night, tossing and turning in her bed, her body on fire for his touch. She realised, bitterly, that his devastating kisses had brought back to the surface all her carefully repressed feelings and emotions.

She sighed. Hugh! Would she ever be free of his fatal attraction? Hugh, who was capable of making her despise him one moment, and herself the next. This heavenly island could have been paradise, but with his serpentine presence, it seemed more like hell.

Running an unsteady hand through her long hair, she glanced at her watch. 'Come on, Tasmin,' she called. 'We're going to be late for lunch!'

Towelling down the child a few minutes later, she scolded, 'Come on, hurry up! We mustn't be late. Austin told me this morning that we've been asked to join your uncle for lunch today.' And a load of laughs that's going to be, she thought in ironic despair.

Driving back to the plantation house, Annabel extracted a promise from Tasmin not to indulge herself in mimicry at lunch.

'Was—was Uncle very cross?' Tasmin asked unhappily.

'No, of course not,' Annabel said soothingly, 'but as

you can imagine, he wasn't very pleased either. So
don't do it again.'

'I'm truly sorry, Annabel,' the little girl said with a
sniff.

'I know you are, sweetheart. Let's forget it, shall
we?' Annabel put an arm about the small, slight figure
and gave her a hug.

'Oh, I do love you, Annabel. Lots and lots ...'
Tasmin laughed happily, throwing her arms about her
new governess.

'Hey, watch out! I'm supposed to be driving this
thing!' Annabel laughed, deeply thankful for the
comforting presence of such a lively and engaging
child. 'Quick, run along to Hannah and change,' she
said as they entered the house and ran up the stairs.
She hurried into her own room, conscious of the
particles of sand still sticking to her legs and arms. A
quick shower and a change of clothing made her feel
much fresher, and still on the trot, she collected
Tasmin and they sped downstairs. 'Just made it,' she
muttered, as the gong sounded and they went slowly
into the dining room on its last stroke.

Austin had been emphatic that morning that His
Lordship demanded absolute punctuality, and although Annabel had no idea why they had been asked
to lunch with Hugh, she was determined not to give
him any cause for complaint. She was still feeling
shattered from their encounter of late yesterday
afternoon, and it would be almost as much as she
could manage to stagger through lunch, without the
addition of an argument about her late arrival.

She ate her lobster slowly, in silence, as Tasmin
chattered away to Hugh about their morning on the
beach. He had greeted their arrival in the dining room
with bland politeness, and although she still felt
awkward and nervous, he had, fortunately, not

addressed a word to her so far.

Annabel became absorbed in a tricky piece of dissection of the lobster's claw, as Tasmin started on a long and involved story about something Hannah had said, and only looked up as she heard Tasmin complaining, 'You haven't been listening to a word I've said, Uncle!'

She raised her head to find Hugh's concentrated gaze bent upon her, and was unable to stop a blush spreading across her features. Furious with herself for responding in such a way, she was further enraged at the way her hands trembled as they raised the glass of water to her lips. You silly fool, she told herself contemptuously, he must think you're an idiot!

It was not possible to guess what Hugh thought, as impassively he rang the bell for the next course.

'Oh, please, please say you'll take us!' begged Tasmin.

'Take you where?' asked Hugh, giving her his full attention.

'Honestly, Uncle! I've been telling you all about it. Hannah has told me about the animal flowers in the cave at North Point. Please can we go tomorrow and see them?' pleaded Tasmin.

'Tomorrow's no good. It's Sunday—house opening day,' replied Hugh, and the child groaned theatrically. 'However, I've got to go and visit a farmer on some of my land at Crab Hill this afternoon. As it's only a mile away, I'm prepared—as an enormous favour—to take you today.' He laughed as Tasmin leapt from her chair to give him a huge hug.

A spontaneous longing to take the child's place in his arms swept over Annabel with enormous intensity. She blushed again for the second time that day, horrified and ashamed that she could still be so attracted by a man who obviously cared nothing for

her—and never had, she reminded herself. Looking
up, she saw Hugh's sardonic glance sweeping over her
flushed features. I bet he can read my mind, she
thought gloomily, stabbing her chocolate soufflé
viciously with a spoon.

As they set out in one of the estate Land Rovers,
Tasmin explained that the 'animal flowers' were, in
fact, sea worms. 'Ugh!' said Annabel, involuntarily.

'Don't be silly,' retorted Tasmin, from the back
seat. 'You'll love them; they don't look like worms at
all. Hannah says they look like a carpet of coloured
flowers. Hannah says that they're "*unique*".'

'Hannah says . . .!' commented Hugh with a dry
laugh, turning to smile at Annabel, who gave him a
faint, nervous smile in return. Dressed for the outing
to the cave in a sleeveless white blouse tucked into a
slim pair of jeans, she found it strangely disconcerting
to find herself sitting so close to Hugh. Close enough
to smell his musky aftershave, and for their bare arms
to occasionally touch as he worked the gear lever up
and down. The narrow roads and hairpin bends might
have made the frequent changing of gears necessary.
She was not, however, convinced that he had to drive
quite so furiously, jerking the car around the bends
the way he was doing. Although she looked studiously
ahead, she was conscious of his grinning amusement
each time their shoulders touched, as he swung the
wheel this way and that.

Hugh dropped them off, and waving cheerfully, said
he'd be back soon. Annabel and Tasmin picked their
way over the rocky terrain, and looked about them.

Well named, North Point was indeed the northern-
most tip of the island; and as they peered over
the edge of the cliff, the raging waters of the Atlantic
Ocean presented an awesome sight. Breaking with a
clap of thunder over the granite rocks, the spray from

the waves bounded up hundreds of feet into the air. The noise was deafening, and Annabel and Tasmin had to communicate their wonder at the sight in sign language.

They made their way towards a nearby café, battling against the strong easterly winds that whipped Annabel's long hair around her head, making her wish she had brought a headscarf.

Inside the café, they settled for a cool lime squash each, and made enquiries about the animal flowers. The man serving them pointed out a large rock formation by the cliff edge where some native boys were selling locally-made crafts. 'It's over there,' he said. 'But do take care, it's a narrow climb down to the cave.'

Tasmin could hardly wait and dragged a protesting Annabel, who would have liked more time to finish her drink, over to the large rocks.

The boy in charge took their entrance fee, and Tasmin quickly disappeared from view, accompanied by a young boy with a flashlight.

I wish I'd never got involved in this—I must be mad, Annabel said to herself, as her hands touched the wet walls of the cave entrance. The steps wound around and around, and she was moving steadily downwards, when she heard Tasmin give a shout. Startled, she gave a little jump, missed her footing on the rock steps, and slipped forward.

She didn't go too far, her left foot becoming wedged under a protruding rock, and she cried out at the excruciatingly sharp pain radiating from her ankle. Tasmin and the boy came galloping back up the steps towards her, the boy's torch still on.

'Oh, Annabel! Are you all right?' cried Tasmin anxiously.

'Yes, I'm fine,' she said, gritting her teeth and

trying to sound as normal as possible, in order not to
upset the child. 'I've just been silly and slipped and
twisted my foot,' she explained. 'Can you get by me
and go and ask the man at the cafe to help me out?'

Tasmin ran off, leaving the boy, who squatted down
making soothing noises at Annabel in an effort to
comfort her. She was, in fact, more grateful for his
torch, which lit up the surrounding walls, helping to
keep the inky darkness at bay. She tried to thank him
for remaining at her side, but the pain was becoming
worse and she found it difficult to concentrate.

It wasn't long before she heard the cheerful voice of
the café owner approaching, and when he could hear
her, she explained what had happened.

'I think I'm stuck!' she yelled, and heard the man
speaking rapidly to the boy beside her, who replied so
fast in the local sing-song dialect that she couldn't
follow a word he said. There was silence as she heard
the man above climb back to the surface, and she
thought with despair that she had been abandoned.

She didn't know how much time had passed when
she heard footsteps again, and a familiar voice
grumbled, 'Can't leave you alone for a minute, can I?'

'Oh, Hugh!' she cried, and burst into tears. 'I'm *so*
glad you're here!'

'Well, I'm not. What a bloody awful place!' He
squatted down by her head. 'Now just lie quietly, and
we'll get you out as quickly as possible.' He spoke
rapidly to the boy and slipped his hands under her
shoulders. He pulled while the boy pushed, and
together they got her to the surface.

Looking at her limp form and chalk-white, tear-
stained face, Hugh scooped her up in his arms and
carried her over to the Land Rover. A subdued
Tasmin already had the door open, and he placed her
as carefully as he could on the back seat.

'This isn't going to be a comfortable journey,' he told her. 'But be a good girl and grin and bear it. I'll get you home as soon as I can.' He was right, it wasn't a pleasant journey, with her foot aching and throbbing. She did notice, however, that quite differently from their outward journey, Hugh drove as carefully as he could down the winding roads, causing the car to swerve as little as possible.

At last they arrived back at the plantation house, and Hugh lifted her gently out, carrying her indoors through the throng of chattering, concerned servants. 'Lucky for you I'm fairly fit,' he smiled down at her, as he mounted the stairs with her still lying in his arms.

Despite her throbbing foot, she trembled, as she felt the steady beat of his heart, and the warmth of his skin through his thin cotton shirt.

He placed her carefully on her bed, and shooing Tasmin and all the curious servants out of the room, commanded Josie to bring up a bowl of hot water, and the first-aid box. Lying back on the pillows, Annabel watched as he disappeared into her bathroom, appearing again a moment later with a towel.

'Unzip your jeans, and I'll just pull them off.'

'What? I . . . there's no n-need to b-bother . . .' Annabel stuttered confusedly. 'I'm sure my foot will be fine—really.'

'Come on, Annabel, let's not have any nonsense!' Hugh stood at the end of the bed, his hands on his hips in a commanding stance. 'Your trousers have to come off, so I can look at your foot and ankle properly.' As she still hesitated, he threatened her, 'Either you undo your zip, or I will!'

Lying flat on the bed, looking up at his determined and forceful expression, she reluctantly did as she was told, arching her back to enable him to pull her jeans off. Settling back down on the bed again, she winced with pain.

His sharp eyes caught her expression. 'What's the matter?' he asked quickly.

'It's my back . . . it's very sore.'

'Undo your blouse and roll over,' he said. 'I'll take a look at it.'

Annabel blushed furiously as she looked down at her long legs, only topped by a scanty pair of briefs. Hesitating, she looked up and meeting Hugh's mocking eyes, blushed again with embarrassment.

'I'm glad you find this amusing,' she muttered angrily, as her nervous fingers fumbled with the buttons of her blouse.

'Well,' Hugh drawled mockingly, 'I must admit that the sight of your maidenly blushes does strike me as somewhat ridiculous!'

'Ridiculous . . .? What do you mean?' she demanded angrily, as she finally managed to undo her blouse, and turned over on the bed for his inspection of her back.

'I meant nothing,' he said soothingly, trying to lift the back of her blouse. 'I'm sorry, Annabel, you'll have to take your blouse off, the graze seems to be near the top of your back, and I can't reach it.'

'Oh, for heaven's sake!' she groaned with exasperation, sitting up again and trying to wriggle her arms out of the tight blouse. 'I know what you meant,' she said accusingly to Hugh as he bent to help her, the touch of his hands inflaming her nerves, already raw with tension. She blushed again, and trembled as she remembered their lovemaking in the past.

He gave a deep throaty rumble of laughter as he looked down at the struggling girl, accurately reading her mind.

'You bloody man!' she hissed, her face flaming with

fury. 'Let me tell you I don't make a habit of . . . of undressing in front of a man. At least,' she taunted him unhappily, her voice rising unsteadily, 'at least, thank God, I'm not like all the rest of your girl-friends—my lord. Obviously . . . obviously they're used to stripping at the drop of your hat!' She turned over on her stomach, burying her face in the pillows with a sob.

Hugh sighed. 'Oh, Bella, don't be so silly . . .' he said softly as he gently unhooked her bra. 'You've grazed your backbone quite badly, probably when you slipped and fell down the cave steps. Now lie still, there's a good girl, while I smooth on some ointment.'

At that moment Josie came into the room with a tray containing a bowl of hot water and the First Aid box. She put it down and left, giggling probably to regale the rest of the house with the fact that the master was putting ointment on the governess's bare back, thought Annabel gloomily.

Hugh took a jar of salve out of the box. 'It may sting, but grit your teeth, Bella. It will soon wear off.' Thankful that her face was hidden from his gaze, she relaxed under the gentle touch of his fingers. It did hurt a bit, but not enough to dispel the feelings of warmth and languor engendered by his touch.

'Right, you can turn over now,' Hugh's voice broke into her thoughts. 'Let's have a look at your foot.'

She turned over gingerly, and lay back quietly with her eyes shut, clasping the loose bra to her breasts, as he bathed her ankle and bound it tightly in a crêpe bandage.

'It's going to be all right, I think, Bella,' he said quietly, standing beside the bed, looking down at the pale girl. 'I'm sure you've only twisted your ankle,' he added, 'but I'll have the doctor over to look at it tomorrow.'

'Can I please have my . . . my nightdress?' she asked in a small, embarrassed voice. 'It's hanging behind the bathroom door.'

'Do you want any help?' he asked, the mocking light back in his eyes as he handed her the froth of white silk.

'No . . . no, I don't!' she gasped, trying to rise, and wincing at the pain.

'For God's sake, Bella, stop behaving like a fool!' he barked angrily, and helped her to sit up. Over her muffled protests, he swiftly removed the bra from her nervous fingers and slipped the nightdress over her head, easing it down over her raised arms.

'Now, is there anything else you *don't* want me to do for you?' he asked with lazy amusement as he sat down beside her on the bed.

'No . . . I—I'm very grateful for everything. I—I'm sorry I was so rude just now . . .' Annabel's voice died away as he gently stroked a damp tendril of hair from her forehead. His touch, so warm and tender, was almost more than she could bear, and she shut her eyes to hide the tears that threatened to flow at any moment.

'It was a nasty experience, but you'll feel better soon. I'll tell Josie to bring you in a couple of aspirins, that should help. Rest now, I'll see you later.' Her eyes flew open as she felt him gently touch her cheek, surprising a warm, soft look in his eyes, quickly masked beneath his heavy eyelids, as he got up and swiftly left the room.

Annabel awoke some hours later, to find Josie turning on the lights and drawing the curtains. 'Massa coming now,' she said with a giggle as she left the room, her place being taken a minute later by Hugh who appeared with a glass in his hand.

'I'm not sure if it's exactly the right medicine for

invalids, but I thought a brandy and soda would be welcome,' he said blandly, sitting down on the bed beside her.

Raising herself up carefully, she took the drink from his hands. 'I—I feel much better now,' she said with a nervous shiver, as he bent forward to lift and replace a strap of her nightgown which had slipped down her arm.

'I'm sure, as I said, that your ankle is just twisted, but the doctor is coming first thing in the morning, so don't try and walk on it till he's been.' His voice was firm, his eyes enigmatic, as his hand slipped slowly down from her shoulder to stroke the soft skin of her inner arm.

Annabel's heart began to beat rapidly. 'I—I haven't thanked you for all you did. I was so frightened that I'd be stuck in that cave for ever ...' she said breathlessly, lifting her drink with a trembling hand and burying her nose in the glass to cover her confusion.

Hugh was wearing a black silk shirt, unbuttoned at the neck displaying the strong column of his throat, the soft material closely moulded to his broad shoulders and strong, muscular arms. Lying back against the soft pillows, Annabel felt faint as the overpowering masculinity of his dark figure assailed her senses.

He had been so kind and rescued her from that appalling cave, so she really couldn't tell him to go away. But how she wished he would! The way he was gently stroking her arm, and the gleam in his grey eyes ... She found difficulty in breathing, as the warmth of treacherous desire invaded her veins.

'I—I think I'll just go to sleep again now.' Annabel moistened her lips, which had suddenly become dry and parched. 'I expect that ... that you'll want to get dressed to go out. I mean ...' she broke off, as he removed the glass from her trembling hand, his eyes gleaming with amusement at her obvious confusion.

'No, I'm not going out tonight. So if you want me, just ring your bell.' He smiled sardonically as her face flushed at the *double entendre* in his words.

'I ... er ... I don't ... won't ... want you,' she said as firmly as she could, the husky note in her voice betraying her tension.

'You seem very certain,' he drawled, as she tried to ease herself down beneath the bedcovers.

'I—I am,' she retorted huskily.

'How sad!' Hugh's voice was rich with amusement as he bent forward, brushing his mouth across her trembling lips. 'Goodnight, Bella,' he whispered, his lips moving softly over hers with a teasing sensuality that caused the blood to pound in her veins.

With a herculean effort she managed to tear her mouth away from his, burying her flaming face in the pillows. 'Leave me alone!' she gasped. 'Why—why don't you go and see your girl-friend? I'm—I'm sure she'd welcome your attentions—which is m-more than I d-do!' Her tightly clenched eyelids were unable to prevent a small tear from trickling down her flushed cheek.

'Oh, for God's sake!' Hugh groaned, the lines of strain deepening about his mouth.

'Just go away!' her cry was muffled as she tried to burrow deeper into the soft pillows.

There was silence for a moment, followed by a strangled curse and the click of the door as he quietly left the room.

CHAPTER FIVE

ANNABEL awoke to yet another glorious day. The morning sun, slanting through the windows of her bedroom, emphasised the mellow glow of the wooden panelling. The blue silk curtains fluttered in the morning breeze, and on the windowsill, waiting for their usual crumbs from her breakfast, were the little yellow birds, about the size of a large wren.

She had asked Josie what they were called, and the girl had replied that her cousins, who occasionally visited Josie's family from their home in the Virgin Islands, called them Bananaquit. 'Maybe 'cos they's so yellow,' she said, and laughing had added, 'but lordy, do they like sugar!' They certainly did. Annabel had experimentally put a few grains out on the windowsill and been amazed by the resultant cloud of yellow, chattering birds that had descended.

As she lay in her bed looking out over the birds, at the top of the dark cedar trees beyond, and smelled the flower-laded scent on the soft breeze, she sighed deeply. Her head felt muzzy and her foot and back were still uncomfortable. It could have been much worse, of course, but thanks to Hugh's prompt rescue ... She tried to check her errant, wayward thoughts, and failed miserably.

She could still feel the comfort of his arms about her as he had so lightly carried her upstairs, his soft touch on her brow, the tantalising promise of his kiss. Sighing deeply again, she gave way to despair. He just felt sorry for you, like he would for anyone who was hurt, she told herself unhappily. He doesn't care a hoot about you—and what's more, he never did!

It seemed almost unbelievable that a summer romance could have changed her life so irrevocably. Many of her friends seemed to fall in and out of love quite happily, skipping through life with little or no damage to their emotions. Why couldn't she have been like that? She had only fallen in love once in her life, and it seemed as if she was marked for all time.

Hugh had never really loved her. Lust? Oh yes. But not love—not as she understood the emotion. He had made it quite plain in the drawing room, on the day of her arrival, that it was his wife he had loved all the time, not her at all. You were nothing but a summer's diversion, she told herself bitterly. Just a pretty girl with whom he had amused himself . . .

It wasn't as if she hadn't been warned, she remembered, moving restlessly against the pillows. Her friend Mary, who had been working in the P.R. Department of the London auction house, helping to produce the glossy catalogues and advance notice of sales, had been blunt and down to earth. She had pointed out that super as Hugh Grey was—and after catching sight of him one day she had to admit that he was the best-looking man she had ever seen—nevertheless Annabel didn't seem to know much about him. Why hadn't she met any of his friends? What did she know about his relatives? 'Watch out, Annabel,' Mary had said soberly.

Annabel had merely laughed, secure in the knowledge of her love, and his declared passion for her. She had wanted nothing more than his presence and had been blind and oblivious to all else, as spring had given way to the long hot days of summer.

As time went by, his goodnight kisses had become more fierce, more ardent, and despite her strict

Nonconformist upbringing, for the first time in her life Annabel had been swept with an overwhelming desire to give herself completely to the man she loved so much. Over the next weeks tension had sprung up between them, the strain of not being able to release their passionate need for each other had begun to corrode their relationship. Annabel had grown thinner, day by day, as, racked by great waves of desire she hadn't known she was capable of feeling, she had fought to keep control of her treacherous body.

Suddenly, Hugh's overwrought emotions had seemed to snap, and he had demanded abruptly that she take some days off work. After a brief internal struggle she had agreed, and he had driven her off to a cottage on the south coast. Their three days there, seeing no one and going nowhere, had been a magical experience. Hugh had been a tender, warm and gentle lover, raising her, with shattering intensity, to the heights of sexual fulfilment, while she had responded ardently with all the warmth and generosity of her loving nature.

Hugh drove them back to London very late on a Friday evening, both suddenly feeling hungry as they had driven through the empty streets. 'Come on,' he had laughed, 'we'll go and visit your namesake!' She had looked at him, mystified, until he had arrived outside a night club, Annabel's in Berkeley Square.

After their meal, he had taken her on to the tiny, crowded dance floor and locked in his arms she had shut her eyes, oblivious to the noise, the shrieks of laughter from nearby tables, and the flashing light bulbs of society photographers. Later, as he bade her a fond farewell, promising to see her again on Monday evening, after a business visit to Birmingham, he had asked her to remember that he loved her with all his heart . . .

What heart . . .? Annabel thought miserably, as she looked out at the morning sunshine of Barbados, a small tear trickling down her cheek. All her bright dreams, all her shining love had been crushed to smithereens when she returned to work on the Monday morning. Mary had been waiting for her, and had made Annabel sit down before silently handing her a newspaper.

She had laughed gaily, she remembered, her cheeks had been glowing with happiness, as she looked down at the gossip column, suddenly startled to see a picture of herself and Hugh dancing at the nightclub on Friday night. Quickly her eyes had scanned the newsprint and she had become icy cold and faint as she read: 'Rich young man-about-town Hugh Grey was also at the Friday night bash, with a dishy blonde in tow. Nobody seemed to know her name, but it certainly wasn't his wife, Venetia!'

Still, after two years, Annabel had no clear recollection of what had happened next. She had apparently fainted, and Mary had taken her home in a taxi, making her a cup of tea and persuading her to lie down. As Mary was about to leave, to go back to work, Annabel had suddenly remembered that Hugh was due to meet her after work. 'If he turns up, just give him that newspaper, Mary, and tell him I never want to see him again as long as I live.' Turning a deaf ear to her friend's protests that it might all be a ghastly mistake, she had cried, 'I'm the fool who made the ghastly mistake . . .' before turning her face to the wall.

Later in the day, almost unbelievably, a telegram had arrived from her father asking her to come home as soon as possible as her mother was gravely ill. Still in shock, she had filled a suitcase and boarded a train home to Northumberland. Hugh's betrayal of her love and trust, followed sharply by the news of her mother's terminal illness, had proved to be the worst twenty-four hours of her life. Her father's stroke and death, some months later, had merely served as the coup de grâce to a period of her life which still haunted her dreams, and had now become a living nightmare . . .

Wiping away the tears which were trickling down her cheeks, Annabel gave way to despair and a deep burning resentment at the way life was treating her. It wasn't as if she hadn't suffered. Never once, in the past two years, had a day gone by when she hadn't felt sick with longing for Hugh, full of self-contempt for her foolish innocence. Surely she had paid any debts that were owing? How could the being she regarded as a merciful God have placed her in such a predicament?

It wasn't fair! It was more than flesh and blood could stand, she railed inwardly, lying back on the pillows exhausted and shaken by her memories. Eventually she managed to find the strength to lever herself out of bed, and manoeuvred herself, careful not to put any weight on her foot, over to the bathroom to wash her tear-stained face.

Returning to the bedroom, she found Josie putting down her breakfast tray. 'Lordy, lordy, miz,' she said cheerfully, 'you look terrible! Almost as bad as the master! He's that cross! Whee ... ' she grinned at Annabel, 'he sure got out of bed the wrong side dis mornin'!'

Well, at least it was his own bed for a change, thought Annabel gloomily, remembering how his car had roared off into the night every evening since she had arrived. With a sigh she moved over to sit in the chair, and began pouring her coffee.

Josie started to make the bed, and from behind Annabel, she uncannily answered her unspoken thoughts.

'That Miz Imogen, she ain't no good! Don't you worry none. Austin, he say she's nothin' but poor white trash!'

Oh heavens, thought Annabel in dismay. Hugh was right about the bush telegraph! The servants would obviously take a keen interest in everything that went on in the plantation house—it provided their livelihood, after all. She didn't suppose, now she came to think about it, that the servants had missed the obvious constraint between her and Hugh. She was dying to ask for further details about Hugh's girlfriend, who was apparently 'poor white trash'— whatever that was—but reminded herself fiercely that it was none of her business. It was absolutely nothing to do with her who he went out with, or how he spent his time . . . Nothing at all! She sighed deeply as Josie left the room with a wave, and poured herself another cup of strong coffee, dreading the day in front of her.

The doctor arrived after breakfast, and the kindly old man agreed with Hugh's diagnosis. 'Just take it easy, and rest it today. I expect your foot is sore, but any pain will soon wear off.'

Annabel had just finished dressing in a pair of slim navy trousers and a short-sleeved blouse of the same colour, when Tasmin bounced into the room. 'Hello— you look nice. Are you better? Isn't it a lovely day? What shall we do?'

'Hang on! One thing at a time!' protested Annabel, tying a wide scarlet belt around her waist. 'Isn't it house opening day?'

'Yes, but not till this afternoon. What are we going to do this morning?'

'Well,' said Annabel, thinking aloud, 'it's Sunday, isn't it, so no lessons today. Do you go to church?' she asked.

'Oh yes, I'd forgotten,' said Tasmin. 'We go to a

lovely old church. Uncle Hugh says he's sure the Rector will go to heaven, because his sermons only last five minutes!'

'You're becoming a thoroughly nasty and precocious child!' Annabel tried not to laugh. 'Well, you'd better go and change, and then you can help me down the stairs—I can't stay up here all day.'

Tasmin, in her Sunday best, which consisted of a smart blue dress and a white boater, walked slowly down the stairs, with Annabel's hand on her shoulder. 'Thank you, poppet,' she bent and kissed the girl's cheek. 'Now, you'd better find your uncle. You don't want to be late.'

'Her uncle is here,' said Hugh walking slowly into the hall from the library, and subjecting her tall, pale-faced figure to an intense examination. 'I trust you slept well?' he asked silkily, 'and that your foot is better?'

'Yes ... er ... yes, I'm much ... er ... much better.' She noticed his lips twisting into a grim smile as she floundered nervously. Why can't you be cool, calm and collected? she demanded angrily of herself, as she caught the mocking gleam in his hooded eyes.

'Good,' he said dismissively. 'Now, I'm going to take Tasmin to church. While we're away, you can oblige me by arranging some flowers in the drawing room and the hall.'

'Arrange some flowers?' she asked blankly.

'I have a dinner party tonight, and I feel the house could benefit from a feminine touch. Don't you agree?' he asked, a glint of sardonic amusement in his eyes.

She flushed under his unwavering scrutiny. Why don't you get your dear girl-friend to do the job? she wanted to yell at him. But mindful of Tasmin's presence, she merely shrugged and said, 'I haven't done any large flower arrangements before, but I'll see what I can do.'

'I knew I could rely on you, Annabel,' he drawled mockingly, taking Tasmin's hand in his.

God, I hate him! she ground her teeth, as she watched his tall figure lead the small child down the path towards his car. Josie had been right, she thought thinking about the dark shadows beneath his eyes, the lines of strain in his face. He looks terrible, almost as bad as I feel. Maybe he did go out last night, after all . . .

Annabel pulled herself resolutely together. She had to get through the day somehow, so she might as well attempt to give the house the 'feminine touch' that Hugh had demanded. What a swine he is, she thought miserably, as she went off to seek Austin's aid in the provision of flower bowls and secateurs.

An hour later she stepped back and regarded her handiwork with a dubious eye. I hope he'll approve, she thought nervously, then shrugged with annoyance at herself. It doesn't matter a damn what he thinks, she reminded herself; all she had to do was to concentrate on Tasmin's tuition and fervently hope that he would find a replacement for her very soon.

She was gathering up the sheets of newspaper which she had spread on the drawing room floor to catch any falling leaves and petals, when she heard Hugh and Tasmin return. 'Here I am,' she replied, as the little girl ran into the hall, calling her name with a large bunch of wild flowers in her hand.

'These are for you,' Tasmin said. 'Uncle spent so long talking to people outside the church after the service that I had lots of time to pick these.'

'Not from anyone's garden?' Annabel asked anxiously.

'Oh no—they were in the ditch.'

As she buried her nose in the flowers, savouring their perfume, Annabel marvelled that such beauty could grow in a ditch. What a wonderful island it was! 'They're lovely,' she said, 'and it's sweet of you to pick them for me. I'll just go and get rid of these old papers, and put your flowers in a vase. I won't be a minute.'

Coming back from Austin's pantry, which he had graciously allowed her to use—Josie's wide-eyed amazement at Annabel being allowed into Austin's inner sanctum had given her the only laugh of the day—she found Hugh looking at the flower arrangement in the drawing room.

'This is really very good! Quite exquisite, in fact,' Hugh said slowly, turning to look strangely at the girl in the doorway.

'There's no need to sound so surprised,' she accused him bleakly. 'I copied it from the arrangement in the picture by François Boucher on the wall over there.'

His lips tightened momentarily at her response, as he turned back to view the flowers. 'You've caught the spirit of the painting quite beautifully,' he said in a quiet voice, looking at the sprays of flowering shrubs and ivy, as they trailed down from the vase set in a Sheraton jardinière, which Austin had produced from the attic.

'I was right,' he turned to smile warmly at her, without any of the cynicism that usually marked his expression. 'My home did need the feminine touch, which you've so brilliantly provided.'

Hugh's smile hit her like a blow. Her heart began to thud and she felt quite sick and breathless. The urge to hit back at the man who could so affect her was overpowering. 'Surely your girl-friend can come and give this house her "feminine touch" any time you click your fingers?' she drawled maliciously.

She was pleased to see his eyes flash with anger before he turned away to pull the bell-rope. 'You must try and not be more childish than you can help, my dear Annabel,' he said smoothly, turning back to face her, his eyes blank and unfathomable.

Blushing, she shrugged as nonchalantly as she could, grateful for the appearance of Austin.

'Ah,' said Hugh, 'two Martinis, please, and a glass of orange juice. We're eating outside today, I take it?'

'Yes, my lord,' Austin replied, and smiling at Annabel, he bowed and left the room.

'I see you've managed to wind my butler around your little finger!' Hugh said with a bark of sardonic laughter.

She had to swallow hard not to reply angrily as Austin, accompanied by Tasmin, came back into the room.

'You and Tasmin can take the money at the door this afternoon,' Hugh announced, as they sipped their drinks. 'I'm told the girl who usually does it has to visit a sick mother in hospital.'

'Oh good!' Tasmin bounced on the sofa beside Annabel. 'I like seeing all the people arrive.'

'Yes. Well, I hope your governess will keep a strict eye on you. The last Sunday we were open,' he explained to Annabel with a twinkle, 'dear little Tasmin here, was charging the visitors outrageous sums of money to enter the house. Apparently justifying it on the grounds of "it is more blessed to give than to receive"!'

'Well, that was the sermon that Sunday—and it is for charity,' Tasmin laughingly protested, running over to give Hugh a hug.

'Just keep her under control—that's all I ask,' Hugh grinned, as Austin announced that lunch was ready.

'Oh, how lovely!' was Annabel's involuntary cry, as she entered the enclosed courtyard of what was, in effect, an outside dining room. Ivy, together with pink and white bougainvillaea, roamed in profusion over the grey stone walls, hanging down in fronds that gently moved in the breeze. In the middle of one wall was a lion's head made of stone, water trickling in a constant stream from its mouth into a small semi-circular stone basin below, bright with waterlilies.

The large, round glass table top was set in white wrought iron, with matching chairs covered in pink and white cushions. Against a further wall a long sideboard, of glass and wrought iron like the table, was covered with plates containing cold meats and salads.

'I'm glad you like it,' said Hugh, pouring the wine into their glasses, and giving Tasmin some orange juice. 'It's the first thing I designed when I came here two years ago.' He explained that they always had a cold salad lunch on Sundays, at which they served themselves. 'The servants have enough to do in the afternoon,' he explained. 'Most people are very good, but we have to have someone in every room, to make sure none of the visitors succumb to temptation and lift any of the family silver!'

Annabel ate silently, as Tasmin and Hugh chatted to each other, about the people they had seen at church. Her foot was aching, from standing on it so much to arrange the flowers, and she felt the beginnings of a nervous headache. Peeping up through her long eyelashes, she noticed Hugh's hooded eyes gazing fixedly at her, and she flushed as she looked quickly down, concentrating on her food.

Thank goodness for the wine, it's the only thing that's making this meal at all bearable—that and Tasmin, of course, she thought, as she answered a question from the child. She was a lovely little girl, and she would be very sorry to leave her, Annabel realised sorrowfully.

'Run along, Tasmin. I want to have a word with Annabel about your future tuition,' said Hugh, giving her a kiss as she slipped down from her chair.

'Have ... have you arranged for a new governess?' Annabel asked hopefully, when she and Hugh were left alone.

'Ah ... no, I'm afraid not. Are you so unhappy here, Annabel?' he asked softly.

'Whether I'm happy or not is immaterial. I just want to leave as soon as possible!' she was stung into retorting, upset by the kindness in his voice.

'I thought you liked Tasmin,' he queried gently, his grey eyes expressionless.

'Of course I do!' she burst out. 'She's a lovely child, it's just ...'

'... It's just that you don't feel the same way about me?' he mocked, one eyebrow lifted in cynical amusement.

Annabel brushed a nervous hand through her long hair. 'It's an impossible situation, Hugh, as well you know,' she said quietly, with a sigh. 'However,' she braced herself, 'you wanted to talk about Tasmin's education, which is, after all, the only reason I'm here.'

'Quite correct,' he agreed blandly.

'She's very bright, you know,' Annabel explained. 'Her conversation and general level of intelligence are more suited to a ten-year-old. I'm going to need some more text books very soon.'

'Just let me know what you need and I'll see that it's provided,' he said, getting up from his chair and coming over to assist her to rise.

'I can manage quite well on my own,' she told him breathlessly.

'You look tired and I imagine that your foot is aching,' he said bluntly, 'so don't play the martyr with me, Annabel.'

'I'm not!' she protested angrily, and in her confusion stood on her twisted foot. She would have fallen if his strong arms hadn't held her tightly, as she gasped with pain.

'We'll have to see that you have a stool to sit on by the door this afternoon,' he said huskily, holding her firmly against his hard body. 'You mustn't ... you really mustn't walk around too much ...'

Annabel scarcely heard what he was saying, as he began to gently stroke the hair away from her face, his warm hand moving to cup her soft cheek, as he brushed her trembling lips with his thumb.

'Oh, please—please leave me alone!' she cried, awkwardly trying to twist out of his firm embrace.

'Yes, if you really want me to, Bella?' he said quietly, looking down into her beautiful and confused blue eyes.

'Of course I do!' she snapped, trying in vain to push against his hard chest, averting her face from the hard searching light in his eyes.

'Liar!' he laughed, and swept her up in his arms. 'I strongly advise you not to struggle,' he added in a firm voice. 'I'm merely going to take you back to the house, to avoid you having to walk on your bad foot. I would prefer you not to make an exhibition of yourself in front of my servants. Understand?'

'Yes,' she murmured, hiding her flushed face in his shoulder. She closed her eyes, reluctantly savouring the aromatic smell of his after-shave, the musky scent of his hard masculine body, as he carried her lightly back to the house. Depositing her on a chair in the drawing room, he strode away without another word.

Later, sitting on a stool with a table in front of her,

Annabel was busily engaged in taking the entrance fee of five dollars from the Sunday visitors. Business was brisk, and she also found a ready sale for the illustrated booklets containing details of the plantation house's history, architecture and contents, as prepared and printed by the Barbados Museum and Historical Society.

There was a lull in the arrivals at the house after about an hour, and she was able to look through the booklet, congratulating herself on recognising that the large picture over the drawing-room mantelpiece of a wooded landscape had been painted by Gainsborough. So immersed was she in the booklet that she didn't notice the arrival of a red sports car, looking up only as she heard the car door slam.

Up the path towards her walked one of the most beautiful girls she had ever seen. Small and petite, with a cloud of dark hair surrounding magnolia skin, she delicately picked her way over the flagstones towards Annabel. She was wearing a white sleeveless dress, the top of which clung to her voluptuous figure, while the full skirt fell from a tiny waist and swirled around a pair of perfect legs which ended in tiny feet set in delicate high-heeled shoes.

She was carrying a round wicker basket which she set down on the table. 'Hello,' she said with a drawl. 'You're new here, aren't you?'

'Yes,' said Annabel, feeling like a hippopotamus beside this vision of exquisite, petite loveliness. 'The entrance fee is five dollars, and these booklets . . .'

The visitor threw back her dark head and laughed. 'My dear girl,' she said in a scathing tone, 'I don't pay to enter this house! Where's Lord Lister?' she asked, looking about her.

Annabel was nonplussed for a moment. She couldn't leave her post, and Tasmin, who was supposed to be helping her, was nowhere to be seen.

Just then Hugh arrived in the doorway, and the dark girl ran up to him, putting her hand on his arm. 'Darling Hughie,' she trilled, 'this extraordinary girl expected little old me to pay to see your house!' her tinkling laugh filled the portico. 'Darling, I haven't seen you for a whole week, and you did promise to take me riding ...' she smiled entrancingly up at Hugh, her red lips pouting invitingly.

'Ah ... yes ... er ...' Hugh cleared his throat, 'I've been ... er ... rather busy lately. If you'd like to ride this afternoon, that'll be fine. I'll just go and change.'

'I've brought my jodhpurs and boots,' said the girl, picking her basket up off the table, looking through Annabel as if she wasn't there. 'I can use one of the bedrooms to change in, I suppose?'

'Of course ... er ... darling,' he paused, catching the gleam of contempt in Annabel's eyes. 'You'd be pleased to offer your room, wouldn't you, Annabel?' he asked in a silky voice.

'Of course,' Annabel replied blankly as she watched Hugh put his arm about the girl and lead her into the house. 'Darling,' she heard the visitor drawl as they entered the hall, 'who *is* that dull-looking girl?'

'Oh, Hughie! I'm such a helpless little thing ...' Annabel jumped and turned on her stool, expecting to see the dark girl beside her. Instead, she saw Tasmin's laughing face.

'Tasmin! Your imitations are really going to get you into trouble one of these days,' she said crossly. 'Where have you been?'

'Only to get you some sandwiches, I thought you might be hungry,' the child said contritely. 'Josie is bringing us out a cold drink soon.'

Unable to repress her rampant curiosity, Annabel asked, 'Who was that?'

Tasmin confirmed her worst fears. 'That's Imogen

Harrison. She lives about five miles away. Her father's retired out here, I think. He was "something in the City", Uncle says. I heard Austin and the other servants talking the other day, and they said that Uncle Hugh's her last chance, because two fiancés have run out on her already.'

'Really, Tasmin!' Annabel looked at her sternly. 'You have no right to talk about your uncle's . . . er . . . friend like that, and you certainly shouldn't listen to the servants' gossip.'

'But that's the only way I hear what's going on!' Tasmin grinned at Annabel, who was hard put to it not to smile back at the little girl. 'Don't you want to know what they've been saying about you . . .?' Tasmin giggled.

'No, I certainly do not!' Annabel said firmly.

'It's very nice. They say . . .'

'*Tasmin!*'

'Oh, all right!' The little girl smiled angelically up at Annabel. 'But I can say what I think, can't I?'

'Yes, as long as it isn't rude or disrespectful.'

'Well, I expect Imogen is very beautiful, but I don't like her. She treats me as if I was a baby. She's mad about Uncle Hugh, of course,' she added, tucking into Annabel's sandwiches.

And it looks as if he's mad about her, thought Annabel. And yet—she remembered that Imogen had been complaining that she hadn't seen Hugh for a week. I bet he's got lots of other girl-friends stashed away on this island, she thought angrily. He really is a swine!

There was a clatter of hoofs, and the riders came into sight as they set off from the stables. I hope she falls off and breaks her beautiful neck, thought Annabel, consumed by such a wave of jealousy that she felt faint. Unfortunately, it was clear that besides being quite ravishingly beautiful, Imogen was also a natural rider, looking even better on a horse than she did on her tiny feet, if it was possible.

The afternoon wore on, and as the last of the visitors left, Austin came out of the house and told her he had put a cold drink on the terrace. Gratefully she slipped off the stool, and limped through the house.

Stiff from the afternoon's stint, she relaxed on a lounge chair and sipped the cool, refreshing drink. Clever old Austin, she thought, just the reviver I need. What a day! The peace and quiet of the old house enfolded her, only broken by the faint chatter of Tasmin, as she was bathed upstairs by Hannah.

Dusk was swiftly falling, the scarlet streaks of the setting sun became brighter as the skies darkened around them, and Annabel sighed with contentment. The peace was shattered by the loud slam of a car door, and the roar of an exhaust, as, she presumed, Imogen drove away. She braced herself. Back to reality, she thought bitterly, and sure enough, a few minutes later Hugh arrived with a drink in his hand.

'That was a glorious ride,' he said, smiling at her over his drink, as he stood lounging in front of her seated figure.

'I'm glad you enjoyed yourself,' she said in a neutral voice, glancing briefly up at him through her eyelashes. He looks fantastic, she thought unhappily, as her swift glance took in his open-necked, short-sleeved white shirt and the skin-tight cream jodhpurs that hugged his hips and long thighs, his lower legs and feet being encased in black leather riding boots.

'Yes, I certainly enjoyed myself,' he enthused, as he sank down on a seat near her and stretched his long elegant legs out straight before him. 'Isn't Imogen a lovely girl?' She couldn't see his face in the gathering dusk, but his voice was full of enthusiasm.

'Yes, she is very lovely,' agreed Annabel, feeling miserable.

'I'm so glad you like her,' he said. 'You'll be able to meet her again tonight. I have some friends coming over for dinner, and I want you to join us.'

'That's very kind of you,' she said coldly, 'but I think I'll just have an early night. I feel quite tired, and . . .'

'I can't have made myself clear, Annabel,' Hugh interrupted in a firm voice. 'I said I wished you to attend my dinner party.'

'Are—are you commanding me?' she asked incredulously.

'If you like,' he drawled, getting to his feet. 'I would prefer that you came willingly. However,' he shrugged in the gathering darkness, 'you are in my employ, and as such will do as you're told.'

'Don't be ridiculous!' she laughed harshly. 'I'm no Victorian serf—this is the 1980s, you know!' It had been a long day and she was tired, emotionally as well as physically. With a spurt of anger, she continued, 'unlike you, I haven't been riding around the countryside all afternoon. What about my time off duty—*Hughie darling*?'

Hugh gave a lazy laugh, as she bit her lip in frustration at having demonstrated her jealousy so clearly.

'We'll discuss your time off tomorrow,' he said in a tone that brooked no argument. 'All discussions about the rates and conditions of employment between the management and employees of this estate are held on Monday mornings. That's tomorrow. I will therefore expect you downstairs, in a dinner dress and with a beaming smile—don't forget the smile, my dear Annabel—at eight-thirty on the dot! Have I made myself clear?'

'I . . . I won't be spoken to like that! I . . .' Annabel sprang to her feet, almost choking with rage.

'Just do as you're told.' His voice, silky with menace, came out of the darkness, before he turned and strode away.

Really, she fumed, who in the hell did he think he was? The arrogance of the man! His antediluvian attitude . . . it was positively Victorian! Her journey up the stairs took some time, although her foot was much better, and she was in a boiling fury by the time she reached her room. I really hate and despise him, she raged, as she sat on her bed contemplating Hugh with loathing.

CHAPTER SIX

AN hour later Annabel had calmed down somewhat. She realised that there was nothing she could do, short of a cataclysmic row, which would involve the whole household and, more to the point, thoroughly upset Tasmin. She had no choice but to do as Hugh had demanded and attend his dinner-party tonight—damn him!

Wearily, she walked over to her cupboard. She had nothing to wear that wouldn't look like a rag beside what Imogen was likely to be wearing. Who wants to compete—I certainly don't! she told herself defiantly. Nevertheless, as she looked through her clothes, she remembered her friend Mary's maxim, 'When in doubt, keep it simple', and she drew out one of her new evening dresses. She hadn't particularly liked it in the shop, but Mary had insisted that she buy it. 'Just the thing,' she had said.

With only an hour to go, Annabel washed and blow-dried her hair, which because of its length always took a long time. Glancing at her watch, she saw she only had fifteen minutes to dress and be downstairs. He can just cool his heels, she thought, still fired by resentment of Hugh's treatment as, despite her brave words, she hurriedly climbed into her dress and stood in front of the mirror.

It will have to do, she thought, as she tried to bring her newly-washed hair into some sort of order. Applying her mascara, she jumped at a loud knock on the door.

'Overture and beginners, please. Three minutes to

go!' Hugh called out as she heard his footsteps continue on down the corridor.

'Oh, very funny!' she said bitterly, as she finished applying her make-up and left the room. This is going to be a terrible, terrible evening, she told herself gloomily, walking down the stairs and across the hall.

Hugh turned around from the window and stood staring at the tall, slim girl as she stood poised for a moment in the doorway of the drawing room, before going slowly over to the fireplace, the silver dress of pure silk shimmering in the soft lamplight.

Her shoulders, bare save for the tiny silver sequined straps, gleamed above the low-cut bodice moulded tightly to her body as far as her hips, where the skirt, cut on the cross, fell away in gentle folds to the floor. The colour of the dress exactly matched the moonbeam glow of her long flowing ash-blonde hair, and as she stood with flushed cheeks and blue eyes sparkling with anger, she looked elegant, regal and very, very beautiful.

Hugh's hard grey eyes were unfathomable, as he walked slowly towards her. His white evening shirt, topped by a black bow tie, fitted his broad shoulders and long torso like a glove, contrasting sharply with his deeply tanned face, while a black silk cummerbund clasped his waist over slim, well-cut black trousers. He—he looks sensational! Annabel thought breathlessly, as he stood in front of her.

'Almost perfect,' he drawled. 'There's just one thing wrong, though . . .'

'What's that?' she asked, looking anxiously down at her dress.

He cupped a hand under her chin, raising her face until it was a few inches away from his own. With his thumb, he gently stroked the side of her mouth.

'My dear Annabel,' he purred, his face creasing into a mocking grin, 'where's the smile? I particularly remember commanding a beaming smile.'

As his cool grey eyes regarded her lazily, and his thumb continued to stroke her mouth, she began to tremble violently. Breaking away, she went to stand with her back to him, staring blindly at one of the paintings on the wall, as she struggled to regain her composure. The sound of cars arriving, broke the silence.

She whirled around to face him. 'You, *my lord*, will have to command someone else! As you yourself said, negotiations take place on Monday mornings,' she glared at his handsome face with defiance. 'As a paid-up member of the National Union of Teachers, I have the pleasure to inform you that today is Sunday!'

'Ah, Annabel,' he laughed softly, his eyes gleaming dangerously. 'We have a bargain—Monday morning it shall be!' He laughed again as he went forward to greet his guests.

'Rosalie,' he said, ushering the new arrivals into the room, 'allow me to present Tasmin's new governess, Miss Annabel Wair.' Annabel looked with astonishment at a woman who, broad as she was tall, was dressed in a purple caftan and was—amazingly—wearing a purple wig to match her dress.

'Annabel, this is Mrs Rosalie Hunt,' Hugh turned to the man who had just entered the room, 'and this is her son Brett . . .'

'Save your breath, buddy boy!' laughed the American she had encountered at the airport. 'Annabel and I have already met!' He took her hand and bent forward to kiss her cheek. 'I'm moving in fast, just in case you disappear again before I've had a real chance to get to know you,' he said, beaming down at the beautiful girl.

'Hello, Brett,' Annabel smiled back at him. She was still feeling upset by Hugh and grateful to know someone at the party.

'Come over and meet my mother—she's going to love you,' he said, as she allowed herself to be led across the room, with Brett's friendly arm firmly around her waist. She was pleased to see Hugh's eyes darken momentarily, his mouth tightening into a firm line at Brett's obvious admiration.

'This is the girl I was telling you about, Mom. The one I met at the airport.' Soon she was chatting away happily to the Hunts about Tasmin's progress. Brett wanted to know where she had gone, and what she had done since she had arrived on the island.

'Well, I've been to the beach a few times, and to Bridgetown, of course . . .'

'But, honey,' the amazingly huge Rosalie cried in horror, 'you've been nowhere! I can see I shall have to take a lovely girl like you in hand!'

'You've had it now, kid,' joked Brett. 'Run while you've got the chance!'

As Austin came up with a tray of drinks, she looked around the room which was beginning to fill up with the rest of the guests.

'Excuse me, Mrs Hunt,' she said, 'but I don't know anyone here tonight. Could you tell me who they are, for instance?' She nodded at a very handsome West Indian man and his wife, talking to a distinguished grey-haired couple.

'Well, honey,' said Rosalie with relish, 'you've *certainly* asked the right person! Take it from me, if I don't know them, they sure aren't worth knowing!' She hitched up her formidable bosom, and continued, 'Well, the elderly Britons: He was a High Commissioner on one of the Caribbean islands, and when he retired he liked it so much out here he came back to live permanently in Barbados. They are very nice, gen-u-ine people, you'll love them!'

Rosalie was clearly enjoying herself. 'The young West Indian is a bright young member of the Government. I can't remember whether it's finance or . . . never mind . . . He's really cute! Oh boy, is he smart! and his wife is a big noise in a local charity for orphaned kids. Isn't she pretty? I'll introduce you later.' Rosalie Hunt continued to put Annabel in the picture, with cameo portraits of all the guests.

Brett, having finished his conversation with the man standing next to him, turned and smiled at Annabel, 'You've made a great hit with my mother.'

'Well,' she said, 'I think she's marvellous! Amazing—but marvellous! I mean,' she struggled to find the right words, 'she really loves "people", and she's so nice about everyone. She never says anything unkind.'

'Well, certainly nobody could ever say anything unkind about you, honey. I think you're gorgeous!' Brett smiled warmly down at her as she flushed slightly at his words. 'Say, have you always been a governess?'

Annabel explained that she had only been teaching for the last two years, and told him about her previous job in the London auction house. From there, they went on to talk about art and music, interrupted by the arrival of Hugh with his arm about Imogen.

'In all the years of our friendship, Hugh, I've never known you to behave so badly!' Brett grinned at his old friend. 'What a dog in the manger you've turned out to be! Lovely Annabel tells me that she's been here in your house for a week, and has only been allowed out twice to go to the beach.' He shook his fair head sorrowfully, turning to look appealingly at the two girls. 'Now I ask you, ladies, is it fair? Is it right? I can see why Hugh would want to keep this lovely girl to himself—but what about us other guys?'

'I wasn't complaining ... I mean, I didn't say ...' Annabel explained nervously, as Hugh's eyes flashed with annoyance.

'*A week* ...?' Imogen, ravishing in scarlet frills falling from her bare shoulders, regarded the tall girl in front of her with angry eyes, her shrewd mind adding two and two and clearly not happy with the resulting answer.

'I agree, Imogen,' Brett laughed. 'It's nothing short of disgraceful. My mother was very shocked! However,' he said, raising Annabel's hand to his lips, 'I intend to see that for the next month at least, Annabel's life here in Barbados is one round after another of pure dissipation!'

'She does work here, you know,' Hugh drawled, his bland voice at variance with his stiffly held figure and the firm, angry line of his mouth, as he regarded his old friend with stony eyes.

'All work and no play ...?' murmured Brett, placing an arm about Annabel's waist and smiling cheerfully at Hugh's discomfiture.

If it wasn't such a mad idea, I'd think they were quarrelling over me, thought Annabel, completely bemused, aware of undercurrents between the two men which she did not understand.

Imogen, her cheeks pink with anger, had no reservations about the verbal exchange between Hugh and Brett, as she looked at Annabel with active dislike. 'Hughie tells me you're Tasmin's governess,' she said, her eyes sweeping dismissively over Annabel's dress.

'Yes,' she replied shortly.

'Fancy being a *governess*! It all sounds too madly

old-fashioned and boring for words! I mean—how grim for poor old you. Still, I suppose being a teacher is about all you can do, and better than nothing!' Imogen laughed gaily, as she tucked her arm through Hugh's, and gave him a smile from what Annabel was coming to think of as her 'goo-goo' eyes.

'Nobody would ever take you for an intellectual, Imogen, that's for sure!' Brett laughed wryly, as he gave Annabel's hand a reassuring squeeze.

'I should hope not!' The dark girl gave an artificial shudder, and leant closer to Hugh, who was regarding Annabel with an unfathomable look in his eyes. 'I'm just so thankful that I don't have to do anything so madly boring as having to earn a living. I do hope,' she said, her voice dripping with spite and condescension, 'that darling Hughie doesn't make you work too hard?'

I'm fed up with this, thought Annabel, whose face was aching from maintaining a polite smile in the face of such bitchery from Imogen. She hadn't wanted to attend this rotten dinner party, and now to have this ghastly and very rude girl shoved down her throat by Hugh . . . It was all his fault, and more than she could bear.

'It's a pleasure to teach Tasmin,' she said quietly. 'As for Lord Lister . . .' She paused and smiled grimly into his lazy eyes, which grew wary under her scrutiny. 'I can assure you, Miss Harrison,' she said in a prim voice, 'that my employer has shown me every attention imaginable, although not always, alas, entirely consistent with my terms of employment. Nevertheless, such consideration, such delicacy, shouldn't go unrecorded!'

Annabel began to feel almost drunk with euphoria, the strains and tensions of the last week seeming to drain away in the heady excitement of at last being able to hit back at the man who had treated her so cruelly.

'One can only marvel, my dear Miss Harrison,' she continued, smiling brilliantly into Hugh's dangerously flashing eyes, 'at Lord Lister's all-embracing and contemptuous coercion of those unfortunate enough to serve under his tyrannical authority. It would bring a blush to even your maidenly cheek were I to relate the full and glorious extent of his concupiscence, his . . .'

'. . . that will do, Annabel!' Hugh said sharply, his eyes blazing with anger, as Brett's laughter ran around the room, and Imogen looked at the two men with bewilderment.

'I don't understand? What was she saying, Hughie?' Imogen looked up puzzled at Hugh's face, dark with fury.

'I'd say that Annabel here,' drawled Brett giving her a beaming smile, 'was not only displaying a remarkable control of the English language, but was also,' he grinned at Hugh, 'telling her employer and his girl-friend to get lost! Wouldn't you agree, old buddy?' His tall frame shook with laughter.

'Really? How disgraceful! Why, she's only a servant!' Imogen raked the blonde girl with hate-filled eyes.

Sobering up fast, Annabel suddenly felt sick and frightened as she watched with apprehension Hugh's tall, rigid figure begin to relax as he gained control of his anger.

'You're absolutely right—*old buddy*,' he said evenly. 'One should always encourage one's . . . er . . . employees to speak frankly. Annabel and I have already arranged to discuss her terms of employment, first thing on Monday morning. Isn't that right, Miss Wair?' he demanded silkily, his face bland and expressionless.

Annabel, who had glimpsed the brief flash of terrible anger in his eyes, quickly masked by the swift descent of his deep eyelids, was enormously relieved and thankful that Austin chose that moment to announce that dinner was ready.

'Excuse me,' murmured Hugh, as he led Imogen away, leaving Annabel trembling nervously at the thought of tomorrow morning. What could have possessed her to be so silly? It had been more than stupid to allow herself to be carried away like that—it had been sheer folly. Hugh's revenge was likely to be swift and sure, and she was so totally vulnerable. She had become far too fond of Tasmin to leave the child before a replacement could be found—and Hugh knew it!

She allowed Brett to shepherd her towards the dining room, meeting Rosalie on the way. She was unable to prevent him from telling his mother, with considerable enjoyment, of Annabel's retort to Imogen's snide remarks.

'I love Hugh—he's absolutely divine!' Rosalie enthused, 'but as for dear Imogen—strictly poison ivy, darling!'

Yes, and look how she's wound her tendrils around Hugh, thought Annabel miserably, as she watched him settling Imogen into a seat beside him, as they laughed and joked together.

The candlelight glowed on the polished mahogany of the old table, and the crystal glasses gleamed and sparkled as one delicious course followed another. There was a different wine for every dish, and Austin supervised the meal like a great conductor, as the servants leapt to his bidding.

Annabel noticed that Hugh was drinking fast and furiously. It didn't seem to be making any difference to his behaviour, but the baleful glitter in his eyes as he gazed fixedly at her down the table, served to increase her nervous apprehension. So much so that she could only pick at her food, causing concern to Brett who was sitting next to her.

'Come on, kid,' he said comfortingly, accurately guessing the reason for her loss of appetite. 'Hugh won't hold it against you, he's a really nice guy. Now, I want you to come out to dinner with me tomorrow night. The Merrymen are in town. They're a really great group, and we'll listen to them and dance under the stars. How about it?'

'I'd love to Brett, it—it sounds fun,' she said with as much enthusiasm as she could muster. As the meal progressed, she began slowly to relax, basking in his evident admiration, and comforted by his kindness.

When the last course had been cleared away, Hugh said, 'May I suggest that instead of the ladies leaving us gentlemen to our port and brandy, we all stay here, and have coffee and liqueurs brought to the table? The reason for my request is that I for one am dying to know how Rosalie's arrangements for her ball are coming along!'

Everyone agreed, enthusiastically, and while the coffee was being poured, Brett explained to Annabel that his mother owned Henry Earl's castle, on the south coast.

She looked uncomprehendingly at Brett, and he realised that he would have to explain. He told her, briefly, that his mother, the widow of a Texan oil millionaire, owned an eighteenth-century castle in the south of the island. 'It really is a castle, honey, if you can call a Georgian house with battlements and a drawbridge a castle!' His mother owned quite a lot of land around the castle and he, as a lawyer based in New York, was busy helping her to sort out her investments in Barbados and other parts of the world.

'Be that as it may, my mother just loves people—as you've noticed—and she loves giving parties! So every year she gives a grand ball for charity, strictly invitation only, and charges the earth for the tickets. She's really got them psyched out,' he laughed. 'She's made a career out of knowing people, and the fight that goes on to get invited—you'd never believe it!'

Prompted by Hugh, Rosalie launched forth. 'Well, let's see,' she said. 'Everything is laid on. It should be, since it's taking place at the end of next week. Now, I *know* you're all dying to know who's coming!' Annabel looked with surprise around the table. Rosalie was right—they couldn't wait to hear more. It must be quite an occasion to warrant that amount of attention and interest.

Rosalie continued. 'I'm not going to give you all my big names. I like to keep a few surprises up my sleeve, but for openers—Maria Hayden and Ty Clint, the film stars, are coming. I've also arranged to fly in the punk group, Fred Disgusting and the Nose-Pickers. They're travelling in the same plane as the Wolfgang Mozart Players . . . so keep your fingers crossed, folks, it could get nasty!'

Despite the general misery of her evening, Annabel couldn't help giggling, as she caught the twitching shoulders and grinning face of the young black Government Minister sitting opposite. They both had difficulty in bringing themselves under control, as Rosalie continued her catalogue.

'Now let's see. There's Prince and Princess Henri of Meckelburg Zwifelhaven; *her* cousin, the Duke of Plaza, and *his* niece Countess Reveski, who is insisting on bringing her boy-friend, Micky Studd. I wasn't too happy about that, I can tell you—why, he's only a boy of twenty-one—but it turns out he's a hairdresser, so I said O.K.!' She paused as a roar of laughter went around the table. 'You may laugh, but it will be very handy to have someone to do the guests' hair at the party! Oh, darlings, I'm having such fun! I've got heaps more coming, you'll be amazed! I've even got the head of the Italian Mafia—did I tell you all how I met him? He's a real dish! He'll do very nicely for Annabel here. You will come, won't you, dear?' and as Annabel nodded, dumbly, trying to keep her face straight, Rosalie called over to Hugh, 'I'm relying on you to bring this sweet, lovely young girl.'

'Your wish is my command, as always, Rosalie,' said Hugh, with a sardonic laugh.

'But he's taking me!' cried Imogen petulantly, glowering at Annabel.

'That's his little problem, sweetie,' replied Rosalie with a laugh. Turning to Annabel, she said, 'I really meant it, my dear. I expect to see you there.'

'How could I resist the head of the Italian Mafia?' smiled Annabel.

'That's my girl!' said Brett, as there was a general exodus back into the drawing room, for more liqueurs and coffee.

Annabel kept close to Brett and as far away from Hugh as she could, nervously drinking her brandy, more than grateful for its fiery warmth. She was accepting another glass from Brett, when Rosalie gave a shriek.

'For heaven's sake! Isn't that the most fan-tas-tic thing! Hugh darling, who does your flowers? To have copied that picture so exactly—why, it's sheer genius!'

'Mom is a great believer in superlatives,' Brett whispered out of the side of his mouth.

'I asked Annabel to do the flowers for tonight, and I agree with you, Rosalie, that she has achieved a work of art.' Annabel gazed open-mouthed at Hugh's praise, accompanied as it was by a warm, friendly smile in her direction. What's he playing at now? she thought apprehensively, as Rosalie hurried over to sit beside her on the sofa.

'Dar-ling Annabel,' she cried, 'you must—you absolutely must do the flowers for my ball!'

'No—really, Mrs Hunt . . .'

'Call me Rosalie, dear. Mrs Hunt is far too formal when I just *know* that we're going to be *such* friends!'

'Well . . . er . . . Rosalie, I've never really done them before, you know. I mean . . .' Annabel felt overpowered by the sheer force of Rosalie's personality.

'Now, Mom, don't bully the girl.'

'The thing is, honey,' Rosalie confided in a booming voice, 'I've got some really nice, gen-u-ine flower paintings. Why, I see it all now—they're just crying out to be reproduced for my party. The dealer said they were by someone called Jan van Huysum or something or other—I forget. Say, do you know anything about oil paintings?'

'She ought to—she was an art historian when we first met!' Hugh laughed wryly, unconscious of the quick, searching look from Imogen, whose dark eyes narrowed angrily as she realised that Hugh and Tasmin's new governess had known each other before the girl's recent arrival on the island.

'I just knew that this was my lucky day!' Rosalie beamed at Annabel. 'Do say yes, honey! I'm just tickled pink at the idea, I really am!'

Annabel hesitated, then smiled at the large American woman. 'If you're prepared to take the risk of it all being a terrible failure . . . I'll see what I can do.'

'Thank you, darling—I just know that your flower arrangements will be purr-fect.'

'Hughie darling!' Imogen jumped up and ran to put her hand on his arm. 'I'm bored to death with all this silly talk about flower arrangements, of all things. It's such a lovely night,' she gazed winsomely up at him. 'Can't we go for a walk on the terrace.'

'People with small bodies really shouldn't have small, tiny minds,' Rosalie drawled, looking up at the ceiling, as Hugh shrugged, and allowed himself to be led away.

The party began to break up at about one o'clock in the morning, and finally there was only Rosalie, Brett and Imogen left.

'Come on, dears,' said Rosalie. 'It's time to go home. We'll give you a lift, since we pass your door, Imogen.'

'Oh, thank you for the offer, but Hugh and I . . .'

'Nonsense,' said Rosalie. 'It's late and I'm sure he's tired after arranging such a lovely party. Just get your coat, and we'll be off!'

'Hugh!' exclaimed Imogen angrily, but he appeared not to hear her as he talked quietly with Brett, and stamping her tiny foot, she flounced out of the room.

The steamroller effect of Rosalie Hunt proved effective, and a few minutes later Imogen stood meekly in the doorway, waiting to be driven home. 'That's a good girl,' said Rosalie, and turning to Annabel, gave her an enormous wink, as she ushered her son and Imogen out into the night.

Hugh shut the front door, turning to find Annabel about to mount the stairs.

'Not so fast,' he said sharply, a disturbing glitter in his eyes. 'I have something I want to show you.'

'Can it wait until tomorrow, Hugh? I'm . . . I'm really very tired, and it's late,' she pleaded nervously. 'My foot aches, and . . .'

'How can it be aching when you've been sitting down all evening? Come along, Annabel,' he said inexorably, putting a firm hand on her elbow and leading her back into the drawing room. 'What time is it?' he demanded.

'It's one-fifteen,' she said, glancing at the clock on the mantelpiece, and looking at him in surprise.

'Quite right!' he purred menacingly. 'Therefore it's Union negotiation time.'

'I don't understand. I . . .' A glance at his firm jaw and steely gaze, together with his firm clasp of her arm, sent tremors of nervous trepidation coursing through her body. Suddenly short of breath, she tried to avoid his penetrating eyes. 'What do you mean?' she whispered shakily.

'What a short memory you have, my dear Annabel! It's now Monday morning. You told me quite emphatically earlier this evening that as a member of a Union you would only start negotiations on a Monday. Now, I'm a very reasonable man, as you know. Here I am, merely complying with your own request.'

'At . . . at this time of night? You must be mad! What . . . what on earth are you planning to do?' Annabel looked up at him confused and apprehensive.

'I thought you'd never ask!' he murmured, pulling her into his arms, which he clasped tightly about her slim figure, preventing her escape. As she looked up into his eyes gleaming with desire, and felt the strength of his body against hers, she started to shake and feel faint.

'The first step in any Union and management meeting,' Hugh said huskily, 'is to review *past* practices, and that's exactly what I have in mind!'

Annabel's startled cry was muffled as he brought his firm mouth down on to her trembling lips, parting them with ease and ruthlessly ravaging the softness within. His deeply sensual kiss seemed to last for ever, and although she fought him, struggling with all her might, he ignored her puny efforts with consummate ease. As her efforts to restrain him grew weaker, she was betrayed by her trembling and treacherous body. Her fluttering hands buried themselves convulsively in his curly hair as she responded to the flame of desire racing through her veins.

Her body softened and melted within his arms, as his lips became softer, his kiss more tenderly evocative, before he slowly and reluctantly removed his mouth and stood looking down at the dazed girl in his arms.

'Concupiscence indeed!' he said thickly. 'It would seem that your "lustful sexual appetite"—to quote the Oxford Dictionary—matches my own, Bella!'

'Hugh! Please ... I ...' Annabel shook her head distractedly, slow to recover from the assault on her raw emotions. 'I'm sorry, I shouldn't have said—said that.' She took a deep breath to try and collect her disordered thoughts. 'Please let me go,' she pleaded, still held tightly in his arms. 'I—I apologise for what I said earlier tonight to you ... and Imogen. But I ... I really was provoked almost beyond reason,' she protested, remembering his girl-friend's spiteful remarks. 'You're quite safe,' she added bitterly. 'Imogen is so stupid she didn't understand a word I was saying.'

'I'm well aware that your remarks were addressed to me—what an intellectual snob you are, Bella!' he said with sardonic amusement, still holding her clasped tightly to his body.

'Anything is better than being a dumb idiot like your dear girl-friend!' she retorted with contempt, trying to break free of his iron grip.

'Imogen has—let's say—other attributes which I find attractive,' he drawled, his eyes gleaming cynically.

'Yes, hasn't she—and all of them glaringly obvious!'

she snapped. 'It's just a pity her "other attributes" don't include a brain!'

'Darling Annabel, can it be that you are jealous?'

'Jealous? Jealous of that ... that nincompoop?' she panted, still struggling in vain to break his firm hold of her body. 'You're welcome to her. Of course I was forgetting that you find her "restful"—hah!'

'Do you want to know why I find her restful, Annabel?' he said harshly, burying a hand in her long hair and pulling it downwards, forcing her face up towards his.

'I couldn't care less!' she cried, wincing with pain.

'I'll tell you, nevertheless,' he said, eyeing her bleakly, the lines of strain deepening about his wide sensual mouth. 'I find Imogen restful because she demands nothing of me. You took all I had to give, and at the first sign of difficulty, vanished from my sight. After what I had to put up with from Venetia, swiftly followed by your betrayal—I didn't feel I was capable of caring for anyone else ever again,' he thundered angrily.

'That's not true ... I didn't betray you ... I ...'

'Didn't you?' he demanded, his mouth curved into a cruel sneer of disbelief. 'Well, it's all a matter of academic interest now, isn't it? The arrangement I have with Imogen is a far more acceptable one—to me. She wants to marry me, primarily for my title, and I really don't care very much one way or another. It seems a fair bargain, wouldn't you agree?'

'You're hurting me ...' she moaned in pain as his hand clenched in her hair.

'Good,' he said viciously. 'I'd like to hurt you every bit as much as you hurt and wounded me!'

'You're wrong! You don't understand ...' she gasped, as despite his hard words, his hand relaxed its hold. 'I did love you ... I did!' She gazed at him, her blue eyes deep pools of misery, as the tears welled up and began to flow down her cheeks.

'Oh God!' he groaned, sweeping her up in his arms and carrying her over to the wide, deep sofa. 'Bella, my darling Bella—don't cry,' he muttered thickly, as he set her down, putting his arms gently about her once more. His voice was husky, murmuring sweet endearments as he kissed away her tears.

His warm lips moved over her face with light, gentle kisses, trailing down to caress her slim neck before moving slowly up to possess her trembling mouth in a kiss of tender, aching sweetness. Shaken by a swift surge of desire, she gasped, her lips parting eagerly beneath his as, unable to restrain her ardent response, her body moved involuntarily and sensually against his hard figure.

Hugh slowly withdrew his lips, looking down at the beautiful girl, her eyes misty and clouded with desire, as she gazed sightlessly back up at him, the silver haze of her ash-blonde hair fanning about her lovely face and shoulders.

'Bella, my sweet Bella,' he groaned thickly, sweeping the thin straps of her dress off her shoulders and gently cupping her full, creamy breast with his slim fingers.

A great wave of emotion swept through her frame, and she moaned helplessly as his lovemaking became more insistent and demanding. 'No . . . please, no . . .' she whispered, as he undid the zip of her dress, his hands moving over her freed breasts, the rosy tips swollen and taut with desire.

'No . . . stop!' she cried. 'It's wrong . . . it's all wrong . . .' the tears beginning to flow again.

'I want you, Bella—God, how I want you . . .' he groaned, seizing her to him and holding her tightly in his arms, soothing away the damp hair from her fevered brow. 'Don't cry, my sweet love. Don't cry . . .'

'It's all wrong,' she wept, struggling to sit up, her slim frame shaken by great waves of anguish as she broke free of his arms, to stand before him, clutching her dress to her trembling figure. 'It's just lust that you feel! You talk about betrayal,' she sobbed bitterly, 'but I truly loved you, not knowing that you were married—and all you ever f-felt for m-me was l-l-lust!' she cried, and stumbled out of the room, blinded by her tears.

CHAPTER SEVEN

'A DOLLAR for your thoughts, honey!' Brett's voice broke through Annabel's abstracted gaze and she turned to him with a contrite smile.

'I'm sorry, Brett. I was miles away, what were you saying?'

'Well, I wasn't saying it, but I might have been. Here I am, dining with the most beautiful girl on the island, at one of the most romantic night spots—and for all the notice she takes of me, I might be a block of wood!'

Annabel felt ashamed of herself, and hastened to make amends. 'I'm so sorry, Brett. It's just that it seems to have been quite an exhausting day. I'm having a lovely time, I really am. Maybe I'm a little tired, that's all.'

'O.K. kid. How about you and me having another dance?' and he stood up and led her to the dance floor. She gazed around her as they danced, at the glamorous scene which should have delighted her, but which instead left her feeling flat and dejected.

Hugh hadn't followed her as she had sped up the stairs following their confrontation after the dinner party. Achieving the sanctuary of her room, she had leant panting against the door, before locking it and stumbling over to her mirror, where she looked hard at her dishevelled appearance and the passionate desire still evident on her flushed features.

And *you* had the nerve to accuse Hugh of having a lustful appetite! she moaned to herself in disgust. Full of self-loathing, she turned away and moved slowly over to the window to cool her face. Looking out at the starlit sky, with the westerly night breeze fanning her cheeks, she acknowledged her own responsibility for what had happened. She had been about to make the same mistake as she had made nearly three years ago, only this time she had no excuse. She hadn't known, then, that Hugh was married, but now . . .? No one makes love to a girl of twenty-four without her consent, she told herself, sick with shame. And you were certainly consenting!

In those moments of ruthless revelation about herself, she realised that Hugh had been right when he had suggested on the day of her arrival that he hadn't seduced her. He hadn't. Her passion then, as now, had leapt to meet his, and it wasn't only Hugh against whom she had to be on her guard, she reflected bitterly, it was her own self!

Later, as she lay between the cool sheets, trying to sleep and failing to achieve that merciful oblivion, her fevered body writhed in agony. She relived the brief moments of ecstasy she had experienced in Hugh's arms, the all-consuming desire to be possessed by him, and the hopelessness of her situation in the plantation house.

Dancing now with Brett, Annabel looked back over the last three days—three days of unmitigated misery—unable to shed the heavy load of black depression which now seemed to have become her constant companion.

Having fallen asleep at last, she had woken on the Monday morning, bleary-eyed and heavy with dread of the coming day. 'The mister, he gone out early,' Josie had told her as she brought in the breakfast tray, for which information Annabel had been profoundly grateful. Her nervous apprehension had subsided a little, although it took all the resolution of which she was capable before she had been able to join Tasmin in the schoolroom.

The quiet routine had gone some way towards calming her troubled spirits, and when Tasmin had asked if they could take a picnic to the beach, Annabel had seized upon the idea with alacrity. The blessed and uncomplicated relief of the little girl's amusing chatter, and the peaceful surroundings of the deserted beach, had done much to assuage her lacerated emotions, and it was with some measure of fortitude and a more resigned acceptance of her situation that she returned to the house in the late afternoon.

Their arrival had coincided with that of Imogen and some of her friends, who had driven up to the plantation house at the same time as Annabel and Tasmin were walking into the house from the garage.

'Come on, everybody! Darling Hughie will be joining us in the pool later,' the dark girl had called out, as she ushered a glamorous, chattering throng of good-looking bronzed figures through the hall and out into the garden, to the pool. Imogen had totally ignored Annabel and Tasmin, as they stood aside to let the crowd pass.

Only as the last guest had left the hall had she turned and regarded them with large spiteful eyes. 'Just make sure you keep to the servants' quarters,' she drawled at Annabel. 'A governess who doesn't know her place can be an awful bore,' she added with a sickly smile, then spun on her dainty heels and went out to join her friends.

'Isn't she horrid!' said Tasmin, as she led the way upstairs.

'You mustn't say something like that about Miss Harrison,' Annabel managed to reply sternly, in total agreement inwardly with the little girl's sentiments.

'Why not? She *is* horrid, horrid, horrid—and I don't

care what you say—so there!' Tasmin gazed at her mulishly from the landing, her lips trembling unhappily. 'She's just like the wicked queen in Snow White. Austin and the others say she's hoping to marry Uncle Hugh—and when she does she'll ... she'll give me a poisoned apple to eat, I know she will!'

Annabel looked at the child's thin trembling figure, as the grey eyes so like her uncle's began to fill with tears. 'Oh, darling, don't be so silly!' she cried, running up the last few steps and putting her arms about the unhappy child. 'It's been a long day, and you're tired. Now we'll find Hannah, and after your bath we'll have supper together. Would you like that?'

'Oh yes,' Tasmin sniffed, throwing her arms about Annabel's neck. 'I do love you—you won't go away and leave me, will you?'

'Of course I won't, silly girl. Not until your uncle has found someone really nice to take my place.'

'But I don't want anyone else. Oh, Annabel, don't leave me ... please don't leave me!' The tears were now running fast, as the child clung tightly to her neck.

'Come on, darling—a big girl like you, crying?' Annabel wiped the tears away, and lifted the child up in her arms. 'Let's find Hannah. You'll feel much better after your bath. Now what shall we have for supper? Maybe Cook will do us some nice fish, and we can have lots of fattening chips to go with it, hmm?'

Speaking soothingly and not giving Tasmin a chance to say any more, she took her along the corridor and delivered the child into Hannah's warm, welcoming arms. 'Now, be a good girl, and I'll be back just as soon as I've showered off all this sticky sand. All right?' she looked anxiously at the little girl.

'Yes, Annabel,' Tasmin smiled shakily. 'I'm sorry ...'

'There's nothing to be sorry about. You're just tired, that's all. I'll be back in a moment, and after supper I'll read you a lovely long story.' Annabel smiled happily at the little girl, before leaving her to Hannah's tender care. As she walked back along the corridor, the smile slipped from her face, as with a heavy heart she entered her room.

Showered and changed, she stood looking out of her window, her forehead creased with worry. There was no doubt that Imogen didn't like Tasmin, and although she wouldn't be cruel—a poisoned apple indeed!—there was no doubt that she was capable of submitting the child to minor unkindnesses and petty slights. There was nothing she could do, Annabel realised with a sigh. Hugh certainly wouldn't tolerate any interference in his life, and definitely not from her. After last night, he must be regarding Annabel with loathing, and even if she did try and warn him about the antipathy between Imogen and his niece, he would be bound to think it was merely jealousy on her part.

Depressed, she turned and noticed that there was a note for her, propped up on the mantelpiece. She groaned with dismay as she read the telephoned message from Brett, confirming their date for tonight. She'd completely forgotten agreeing to go out with him this evening, she realised, hurrying downstairs to the hall. Frantically thumbing through the telephone directory, she was at last connected with Rosalie Hunt's house and a moment later was speaking to Brett.

'It's all right, honey—I understand,' Brett's voice was warm and friendly. 'There's no need to worry. You see to the little girl, and we'll make it Wednesday instead—O.K.?'

'Oh, thank you, Brett, you are kind ... and understanding.'

'And you thought I wasn't . . .? Oh boy,' he chuckled, 'and there I was thinking that you'd been bowled over by my manifold charms! Have I got a lot of ground to cover! Never mind, honey, see you on Wednesday.'

Annabel had joined Tasmin for supper, and tucking her up in bed afterwards, had looked around for Tasmin's favourite book of the moment, *The Secret Garden*. 'I had it at the beach,' Tasmin said, after Annabel's fruitless search. 'Maybe it's still in the car.'

'All right, I'll just go and get it—and woe betide you if you aren't still in bed when I come back!' Annabel smiled.

She had found the book, and walked back to the house, the evening air filled with sounds of laughter and shrieks of revelry from behind the hedge of the pool. I bet Hugh's having a high old time in there, she thought despondently, as she entered the dark hall, and was therefore startled to hear her name called as she passed the open door of the library.

Her heart thudding nervously, she slowly retraced her steps to find Hugh sitting behind his desk, his tanned features looking strained and saturnine.

'What are you doing here?' His voice grated sharply as he viewed the girl standing hesitantly in the doorway, obviously poised for instant flight.

'I . . . I came down to fetch Tasmin's book. She . . . she wants me to r-read her a s-story,' she stuttered awkwardly, wishing she was a million miles away, and not subject to the scrutiny from such hard grey eyes.

'Surely you were going out tonight? With your new . . . er . . . conquest.' The stern lines of his sensual mouth were grimly twisted into a sardonic smile, the expression in his stony eyes unfathomable beneath their heavy lids. Only a muscle beating in his jaw gave any hint of tension.

'No, I ... Tasmin isn't feeling very ... I thought I'd stay and ...'

'You aren't making a great deal of sense, my dear Annabel,' he drawled. 'Do I take it that Tasmin is ill?' His voice sharpened.

'No. She's just a little upset, that's all.' She turned to leave, anxious to escape Hugh's unwavering hard eyes.

'Wait!' he commanded harshly. 'If Tasmin isn't ill, what's wrong? Why is she upset?'

Annabel felt sick with apprehension. Any moment, she felt sure, Hugh was going to make a reference to last night and ... and she couldn't bear the thought of going through all that again. 'I ... er ...' she shrugged helplessly. There was no way she could explain the problem, not without making it seem as if she was as spiteful as Imogen.

'I'm waiting, Annabel,' he insisted impatiently, drumming his fingers on the desk in front of him.

There was a sound of nearby laughter, as some of the bathing party moved on to the terrace. 'I'm sorry, Hugh. There's no way I can ... It isn't for me to say anything. I ...' She turned her head as the sounds came nearer. 'Surely you should be out there with your guests?' she said distractedly.

His lips twisted into a grim smile as he lifted the gold case from the desk in front of him and slowly lit a cigarette, exhaling the smoke with studied ease. 'What a good question, my dear Annabel!' he drawled with cynical amusement, as Imogen ran past her into the library.

'Darling, why haven't you come out to join us? It's all been such fun, and ...' she turned to follow the direction of Hugh's eyes, glaring at the pale, tall blonde girl standing beside the doorway. 'What are you doing here?' she demanded angrily.

'Annabel and I are discussing matters to do with Tasmin,' he said in a crushingly hard voice. 'Why don't you go and see to your friends? I'll join you in a minute, Imogen.'

The dark girl flushed angrily. 'I must say I find it very boring to always have this—this governess around. I mean,' her tinkling laugh was slightly off-key, 'it isn't as if we have anything in common with her, is it, Hugh?'

Annabel, clutching Tasmin's book tightly in her hands, looked bleakly back at Imogen. Oh yes, we have, she thought bitterly. Hugh Grey, Lord Lister, is exactly what we have in common. Glancing briefly at Hugh, she blushed as she saw his eyebrow lifted in mocking awareness of her thoughts. What a swine he is, she thought, her eyes raking him with contempt, as she turned silently to leave the room.

'Just a minute, Annabel,' he shrugged apologetically. 'Tell Tasmin I'll be up to see her presently.'

'Very well, my lord,' she answered tonelessly. Her legs were trembling as she trailed up the wide staircase trying to ignore the sounds of altercation coming from the library. Maybe she should be pleased that Imogen was being given a rough time by Hugh. However, she was so tired and exhausted by the nervous tensions of the last days, that all she wanted was the blessed oblivion of sleep.

Annabel had just reached the end of a chapter when Tasmin's exclamation of pleasure alerted her to Hugh's presence. She watched as he went forward to sit on the bed beside the child, who joyfully threw her arms about her uncle. The two dark curly heads so close together caused a shaft of inexplicable pain to sear through her body. Silently, she put down the book and quietly left the room.

She did not question the child next morning as to

what had passed between her and her uncle, merely being content to see that Tasmin was feeling much happier, as she settled down to the first lesson of the morning. 'Sums—ugh!' the child groaned with a grin.

'I thought we'd get your favourite subject out of the way early on,' smiled Annabel. 'I was out in the garden early this morning, and picked some flowers,' she indicated the vase on her desk. 'We'll have a lesson in Botany later, and you can draw me some pictures of them as well. Always providing your sums are correct, of course!' she grinned as Tasmin pulled a face.

The peace and quiet of the schoolroom enfolded Annabel, as she sat back looking at Tasmin's head bent over her work. She had spent another restless and weary night, rising early to walk with bare feet on the soft dewy garden lawn. Worries about Tasmin were uppermost in her mind. There was, after all, nothing she could do about her own predicament.

There was so little she could do for the child, she realised with frustration. A replacement for her would arrive any day now, please God. And yet ... what would happen to Tasmin? All she could do was to pray—fervently—that the next governess would be kind and protective. Maybe it would be possible to have an opportunity to warn the new teacher about possible conflict between Imogen and Tasmin?

The thoughts had run like mice hither and thither in her brain, and now, as the child brought her completed work to Annabel's desk, she was no nearer to finding a solution to Tasmin's problem. Giving herself a mental shake, she lifted a small wooden board and knife from a drawer and removed one of the flowers from the vase.

'Now, I'm going to cut across the flower head—so. Can you see ...' The lesson continued, and they were both so absorbed that they didn't immediately hear the schoolroom door open. It was a nudge from Tasmin that caused Annabel to look up to see Imogen standing in the doorway.

'Can I help you?' Annabel looked coolly at the petite vision of loveliness in front of her. How could anyone resist her? she thought with a lump of depression. Imogen, dressed in pale lemon, looked absolutely ravishing, and it was only her hot, angry eyes that spoilt the delicious picture she presented.

'I was just checking that you do actually teach that child,' the other girl drawled.

'She's a very good teacher,' Tasmin sprang to Annabel's defence, before she was able to open her mouth. 'Anyway,' the little girl continued before she could be stopped, 'she knows lots of interesting things I bet you don't know, 'cos you're stupid!'

'Tasmin!' Annabel said sternly. 'That's very rude—apologise at once!'

'No, I won't! I had a long talk with Uncle Hugh last night, and he agreed with me,' she said defiantly. 'He said she was stupid too, he really did!'

'Tasmin, you will apologise to Miss Harrison now. At once!' Annabel commanded.

'Oh—all right,' the child shrugged with bad grace. 'I'm *frightfully* sorry if I chanced to say anything—anything at all out of place, dear Imogen.'

It was only with difficulty that Annabel kept a straight face, as Tasmin so accurately mimicked Hugh's drawl. Looking at the deep flush of fury that swept over Imogen's face, she realised that the little girl had well and truly made an enemy. She put her arm protectively about Tasmin, as the dark girl trembled with rage.

'The sooner that brat is sent to school, the better! You can be very certain, Miss Wair,' Imogen added menacingly, 'that I'm going to arrange your speedy departure from this house!' She turned swiftly and flounced out of the room, banging the door hard behind her.

Tasmin looked with consternation at Annabel. 'I'm sorry,' she said in a small voice. 'I know I shouldn't have said that.'

'It's done now, Tasmin. But for goodness' sake, don't be rude like that again. There's never any excuse for such behaviour, you know. If someone is unkind or rude to you, you must learn to ignore it. It really is far more effective to answer them by turning the other cheek. Do you understand?'

Tasmin nodded unhappily, and since it would be difficult to regain the child's attention, Annabel abandoned the Botany lesson and sent the little girl down to the kitchen for a cool drink and some biscuits. 'Don't be too long,' she warned.

It was, however, about half an hour before the child returned. 'Wherever have you been?' asked Annabel, glancing at her watch.

Tasmin laughed happily, as she took up her reading book. 'Don't be cross, Annabel, but I listened outside Uncle's study. I promise you, I could hear everything he was saying in the hall—it wasn't eavesdropping, really it wasn't,' she assured her frowning teacher. 'He was being very angry with Imogen. He said . . .'

'Tasmin! You mustn't . . .'

'"I will not have my domestic arrangements interfered with,"' Tasmin continued in Hugh's voice, blithely ignoring Annabel's warning. '"You have already—and quite unnecessarily—upset my niece. If it happens again, you will be very sorry." That's what he said, Annabel, he really did!'

'If you've quite finished,' said Annabel with heavy sarcasm, 'I'm waiting to hear you read to me.'

'And then horrid Imogen said, "I'm not prepared to put up with that awful, boring teacher for one more minute—Either she goes or I do",' Tasmin was almost trembling with excitement. 'And do you know what Uncle Hugh said then . . .'

'I've heard quite enough, thank you, Tasmin. Now . . .'

'. . . Uncle Hugh said, "If you wish to terminate our relationship, you have only to say so, Imogen".' Tasmin beamed seraphically at Annabel. 'I couldn't hear any more, but . . .'

'One more word out of you, Tasmin, and I'll send you to your room in disgrace. I can see it's useless to expect you to concentrate on your reading. You can write me a story about what you want to do when you're grown up—if you manage to live that long, which I very much doubt, the way you're going! Now calm down, and get on with it,' Annabel added with a faint smile, unable to resist the child's happy and cheeky grin.

Silence descended on the schoolroom, neither of the occupants finding themselves able to devote their minds fully to the work in front of them, both absorbed in their own thoughts.

By a judicious mixture of early morning schoolwork, and exploration with Tasmin of the island by car, Annabel had managed to avoid Hugh's company. It wasn't until Josie had knocked on her door that evening, to say that Brett had arrived to take her out as promised, that she had descended the stairs to find the two men in the hall.

It didn't need more than a glance to see that Brett and Hugh were on edge with each other. Both of them were being scrupulously polite, of course, but the atmosphere was so thick with tension that Annabel very nearly retreated back to her room, to escape what she felt was likely to be an unfortunate confrontation.

'Brett tells me he's intending to wine and dine you

in style!' Hugh's lip curled contemptuously, as she came down the last few steps.

'How else should one treat such a lovely girl?' the American said blandly, putting an arm loosely around her shoulders.

Hugh's only reply was a snort of disgust as he retreated to his study, shutting the door firmly behind him.

Annabel was still trembling, as Brett handed her into his air-conditioned Cadillac. However, since he occupied the journey in relating some amusing stories about life in New York, by the time they had arrived at the restaurant overlooking the sea, she had managed to get her emotions under some sort of control.

The dance floor was set out under trees containing fairylights that twinkled and shone through the leaves. The gentle murmur of the waves, lapping the seashore in the moonlight, acted as a background accompaniment to the music of the Merrymen, the most popular group on the island, as they played a lilting love song. Brett's right, Annabel thought, this must be one of the most romantic spots on earth. It ought to be a glorious evening, but she felt so apathetic and depressed that it was only by a mighty effort that she smiled and joked with Brett.

The music died away, as they walked back to their candlelit table past the other couples, Annabel looking cool and lovely in a coral pink silk dress. The full skirt broke into swirls over her knees, her lovely tanned shoulders rising from a deep frill on the close-fitting bodice, which emphasised her slim waist. She was glad that she had made an effort and had put on her prettiest dress, she thought, as she looked around her at the other couples gathered there that night.

'You know, you really are a gorgeous girl,' said Brett, taking hold of her hand, as they sat down at the table. 'I'm just sorry that I seem to have come on the scene too late.'

'I . . . I don't know what you mean . . .'

'Oh yes, you do!' he retorted with a dry laugh. 'My old buddy Hugh seems to have got his toe in the door already. Say, how about my challenging him to one of your English duels?'

'Oh, Brett,' she smiled faintly at the thought, 'it's nothing like that. He's got Imogen, and . . .'

'I think it's very much "like that",' he smiled gently at the blushing girl, raising her hand to his lips. 'You knew him before, didn't you? Before coming out here to Barbados, I mean.'

'Yes. I . . . It was a long time ago,' she said slowly. 'I just came out here to teach. I . . . I had no idea he was going to be my employer, you see.' She hung her head unhappily.

'Wow, the plot thickens!'

'The plot—as you say—is every bit as thick and lumpy as a plate of badly made porridge!' she said bitterly. 'It's all been a terrible mistake; coming out here, I mean. I'm leaving just as soon as Hugh can find a replacement.'

'Are you sure Hugh wants you to go? He's been walking around me like an angry tiger. I'd say,' he laughed, 'I'd say that he'd like nothing better than for me to vanish in a puff of red smoke—like the demon king! Honey, the guy's as jealous as hell!'

'Oh no . . .'

'Oh yes,' Brett said firmly, still holding on to her hand. 'However, you mustn't run away with the idea that I'm feeling philanthropic. If he's got himself stuck with the wrong girl, that's his look-out! I just reckon I'll stick around. At least I've got a broad pair of shoulders to cry on.'

'Oh, Brett, you're so nice . . .'

'Nice—hell! Still, it will do for starters, I suppose,' he laughed gently, and raised her hand to his lips again.

Annabel nearly jumped out of her skin as a sardonic voice from behind them asked, 'Is this a private romance, or can anyone join in?' She spun around to see Hugh smiling blandly. His smile did not, she realised, reach his eyes, which remained cold as ice, as he stood looking down at the furiously blushing girl before him.

'The "romance" is coming along just fine, old buddy! Draw up a chair.' Brett stood up, not only to greet Hugh but, as she saw, the rest of the party accompanying her employer. She didn't know the other two couples, but there was no mistaking Imogen, who looked as beautiful as ever. The nervous tremors that had flashed through her at the sight of Hugh settled down to a steady lump of despair, as with much chatter and squeals of laughter, the group joined their table. Animated and excited, Imogen totally ignored Annabel and turned to Brett.

'We've had such a fun evening! We've dined at Alexandra's and then went on to the Pepperpot disco, and now we're here. It's been lovely, hasn't it, darling?' This last was addressed to Hugh. He didn't reply immediately, being busy ordering from the hovering waiter.

He'll always have waiters hovering to do his bidding, Annabel thought gloomily. He's just that sort of person. Damn him, why did he have to come here, of all places? It hadn't been exactly a 'fun evening' such as Imogen had apparently enjoyed, but now it was all spoilt. Overcome with depression and jealousy, she looked with misery at the dark girl's shimmering gold dress and lovely face.

'I think we'll have champagne all round,' said Hugh

to a chorus of appreciation from the other members of the table. 'Make sure it's well chilled, old buddy,' he smiled wolfishly at Brett, before bending swiftly down to grasp Annabel's arm in a grip of steel. 'My dance, I think,' he murmured, as he led her protesting figure on to the dance floor.

'What do you think you're doing?' she demanded angrily. 'I'm here with Brett, and . . .'

'For God's sake, Annabel, just shut up and dance,' he said sternly, leading her to the far side of the floor, beside the waves lapping against the sand.

'I don't want to dance with you,' she snapped. 'You've got a nerve—marching in and spoiling a nice evening . . .' She was suddenly unable to say any more, as Hugh's mouth descended on her open lips in a firm, determined kiss.

'I'll do that again,' he threatened harshly, looking down into her dazed face. 'So I suggest that you keep quiet and just dance—hmm?'

'I hate you!' she hissed, unwilling to cause a scene—as he very well knew, she thought with fury.

'Do you, Bella?' he said softly, smiling cynically down into her angry blue eyes. He put his arms slowly about her and gently drew her closer and closer as they moved to the sensual mood of the music.

Trying hard to keep herself stiff and unyielding, Annabel was unable to prevent her treacherous body from slowly responding to the hard, firm figure pressed so closely to her own. Ripples of excitement began to course through her, as Hugh placed his cool cheek to hers, softly brushing her brow with his warm lips.

As they swayed to the music, he began to lightly kiss her eyelids, and the soft plane of her cheekbone, his mouth moving to brush her lips with a tender, sensual touch that sent the blood pulsing rapidly through her veins. His mouth teased and tantalised her lips until she was breathless, her heart beating like a drum, her body quivering violently in his arms.

Her trembling body brought an answering muffled groan, Hugh's body shaking for a moment, as he clasped her even tighter. Lifting his head, he looked down into her large blue eyes, cloudy with desire. 'What a little liar you are, my love,' he whispered softly, folding her gently within his arms and burying his face in the fragrant cloud of her ash-blonde hair.

They continued to move slowly, totally oblivious of the other dancers on the floor, and it was a moment or two before they realised that the music had stopped. Annabel drew slowly away from Hugh in a daze, as they stood on the far side of the dance floor, trying to pull her shattered emotions together. He took her arm, gently propelling her on to the sandy beach.

She was grateful for the respite. Her legs were still trembling, and she seemed to have trouble with her breathing, as she fought the iron bands which seemed to be constricting her ribs.

'I . . . er . . .' he cleared his throat, looking down at her intently in the moonlight, 'I thought it might be a good idea if—if I got married again soon. What do you think?'

Annabel looked at his tall, handsome figure in a daze. Surely—surely even Hugh didn't have the brass nerve to discuss his forthcoming marriage to Imogen, not when he . . . when he had just been kissing her so passionately? It—it just wasn't possible . . . She must have misheard him.

'What—what did you say . . .?'

'I was asking what you thought about my getting married again.' His voice was quietly bland in the moonlight.

'What do I think?' she gasped, her whole being

suddenly swept by a torrent of misery and pain. 'I think any marriage of yours would—would be a *disaster*, and I feel pity for anyone who took you on—even poor stupid Imogen!' The words came bursting forth, the influence of her Northern childhood evident as she confronted him. 'Oh yes, bonny lad! Just look at you! You've had more girls than I've had hot dinners, and as far as I can see you've got the morals of an alley-cat! You lied and cheated on your first wife, and it looks as if you're busy cheating on your girl-friend. Once a cheat, *always* a cheat!'

'For God's sake,' he shouted, 'you don't understand . . .'

'Understand? I should think I damn well do! Who better? You—you . . .' Her rage, fury and deep humiliation at what she saw as his deliberate arousal of her emotional need for him finally boiled over. Raising her hand, she dealt him a swift, punishingly hard slap on the face, before turning swiftly to run back across the dance floor, seeking refuge in the ladies' cloakroom.

Sitting slumped on a stool, it took her some time to recover from the waves of trembling exhaustion that racked her. Eventually, she went over to the basin to wash her face. She hardly recognised the girl who looked back at her, the greeny-white pallor of whose complexion was surmounted by deep blue pools, swimming with tears.

Looking in the mirror she saw, with sudden consternation, that Imogen had entered the room.

'I wondered where you'd got to. Didn't you enjoy your dance with Hugh, *sweetie*?' the dark girl laughed spitefully, preening herself in the mirror.

'No, I didn't,' Annabel spat back contemptuously, cursing her trembling hands as she tried to dry them on a towel.

'Why don't you go back to England? You know you're not wanted here—by anyone.' Imogen's hot, dark eyes roamed contemptuously over the girl beside her.

'Believe me, I'd like nothing better! In the meantime,' Annabel took a deep breath, 'you can tell your "darling Hughie" to keep his dirty hands off the hired help—*sweetie!*'

If she hadn't felt so awful, she would have laughed at Imogen's gasp of dismay and thunderous look, which boded ill for Hugh on his return to their table.

Walking into the foyer of the restaurant, she met Brett, who was settling their account. 'I'd like to go home now, if you don't mind. I've . . . I've got rather a headache . . .' she said breathlessly.

'Sure thing, honey,' he said calmly, with a swift glance at her white face. 'I'll just finish paying the bill, and then we'll be off.'

CHAPTER EIGHT

ANNABEL wearily jabbed the flower stalk into the twisted chicken wire and stood back to consider the arrangement in front of her, comparing it with the Dutch flower painting behind. This was the third and last arrangement she had to do for Rosalie, and she was fast running out of enthusiasm. Not that she had had much to begin with, she thought glumly, clicking her teeth with annoyance as she removed a wrongly placed flower and re-positioned it correctly.

With a sigh, she bent down and removed some trailing ivy from the almost empty bucket which had, half an hour before, been full of flowers and sprays of foliage. Her back ached, her head was beginning to pound with one of the tension headaches which seemed to be plaguing her recently, and she felt so miserable that it was almost more than she could do to stop herself crying.

'Darling! That's really fan-tas-tic . . .!' Rosalie burst in through the door and stood gazing with dramatic wonder at the nearly finished arrangement.

'I—I haven't long to go now, it should be done soon,' Annabel gave a tired sigh.

'Honey, you don't look too well. Are you all right?' Rosalie came around to look closely at the girl's pale face.

'I've just got a bit of a headache, that's all,' she said with a faint smile, as Rosalie regarded her with concern. 'Could I . . .? Have you such a thing as an aspirin?'

'Of course I have, darling. Now you just take it easy,

and I'll be back with a nice cup of your English tea and some pills. I won't be a moment. You're a really sweet girl to be doing these flowers for me, and I'm truly grateful.'

Left alone, Annabel quickly finished the last touches to the copy of the picture. Not so much a flower arrangement, more a still-life, she thought, fixing with difficulty the large bunch of grapes in the middle of the arrangement. Rosalie had been very efficient, she acknowledged, everything had been ready for her when she had arrived at this fantastic house, late that morning.

Brett and Rosalie had been so kind to her and she was, in fact, grateful for the opportunity to be away from the plantation house and Hugh's baleful presence.

You might have known, she told herself wearily as, her job completed, she sank down thankfully into a comfortable sofa. You might have known that Hugh wouldn't take being slapped, not to mention the awful words she had said to Imogen, lying down. And he hadn't.

She brushed a weary hand through her long hair, as she remembered the aftermath of the dinner-dance. Brett had been kindness itself, driving her home in companionable silence, not asking any questions, and merely dropping her off with a friendly peck on the cheek. Running quickly upstairs, she had stripped off her clothes and fallen into bed exhausted, but not, alas, to sleep.

She had been tossing and turning, miserably unhappy and strung up with nervous tension, when her door had suddenly burst open, and the lights had been switched on. She had sat up, startled, to find Hugh standing in the doorway. One glance at his grim face, his eyes blazing with fury, and she had quailed with terror, nervously clutching the sheets with shaking fingers.

He closed the door softly behind him and stood leaning back casually against it as he looked hard and long at the frightened girl. 'I used to have a quiet life,' he purred menacingly, as he walked slowly over to the bed. 'Not a particularly happy one, I grant you, nevertheless it was quiet.'

Annabel watched him approach, lithe as a panther, and twice as dangerous. Her heart was pounding so hard with fright that her head seemed to echo with its steady beat, as she gazed mesmerised into his hard, gleaming grey eyes. He stood looking down at her as he slowly and deliberately removed his white evening jacket, throwing it down on a chair beside him.

'Ever since you arrived out here,' he drawled with dangerous softness, 'my quiet, ordered and well regulated life has been dramatically changed.' He sat down beside her, undoing his bow tie, and casting it away in the direction of his jacket.

Too late, far too late, she tried to scramble from the bed. Her limbs became entangled with the bedclothes, and he caught her with consummate ease, pinning her arms down on either side of her cloud of pale blonde hair, his eyes gleaming sardonically down into hers.

'Oh no!' His deep, soft laugh was strangely devoid of humour, as she vainly struggled to escape his iron grip.

'Go away!' she gasped tearfully. 'Go away, and leave me alone, you . . . you beast!'

'Beast . . .? Not a very original word, Annabel. Surely with your education you can do better than that? Let me see,' his icy drawl sent shivers of apprehension speeding through her trembling prone figure as she tried to avoid his eyes dark with anger, 'we've had "debauched libertine", and a public reference to what you seem to imagine is my "lustful sexual appetite".'

'I said I was sorry about that. I . . .'

'We mustn't forget, either, your injunction tonight—via Imogen—for me to keep my dirty hands off you, must we?' His voice was harsh as his hands tightened about her wrists like bands of steel. 'Surely, Annabel, you can find a more evocative word than "beast"?'

'Let me go—at once!' she panted, her struggling, twisting figure becoming weaker as she exhausted her last reserves of strength. 'When—when I called you a debauched libertine I—I meant it . . .' she gasped.

'I know you did, you stupid girl,' Hugh ground out the words savagely. 'What interests me is *why*? Apart from the fact that I was still married when I met and fell in love with you, I would be very interested to know what other woman—or women—I'm supposed to have "debauched". Maybe you can tell me? Hm?'

She glanced up at the strong, masculine figure leaning over her, his tanned features looking strained and tense, his eyes gleaming intently down into hers. 'How—how do I know . . .' she muttered, trying to turn her head away from his unwavering stare.

'What I know,' he said huskily, 'is that ever since you arrived out here, my life and my home are fast becoming unbearable. My niece has quarrelled with Imogen; Imogen has quarrelled with me; the servants are becoming upset—for God's sake, even my butler has begun to regard me as some sort of Don Juan! While as for you, Bella—you spit at me like a termagant one moment, and melt into my arms the next!'

'I hate you—I really hate you!' A sob caught in her throat as she tried to glare back at his gradually softening features, the gleaming warmth of desire in his eyes causing her body to tremble beneath him.

'So you keep telling me . . .' he murmured with silky softness, his dark head coming down towards her, '. . . and yet . . . and yet . . .' he breathed, his lips touching hers with feather lightness, his mouth moving gently over her quivering, responsive lips.

'I'll stop—any time you ask me to,' he whispered as he continued to tantalise her lips, leaving her breathless with desire. She could only moan submissively as his kiss deepened, his hands moving to hold her head firmly beneath his caressing and invasive mouth.

'You don't want me to stop—do you?' he breathed, his lips seducing her into a state of helpless trembling rapture. Burying her fingers in his dark, curly hair, she was oblivious to everything except her need to respond to his lovemaking.

Suddenly, shockingly, he had withdrawn his mouth, and a moment later was standing up beside the bed looking sternly down at her, her eyelids still fluttering with desire.

'I suggest, my dear Bella,' he said bleakly, a vein throbbing at his temple, 'that you decide whether you hate me or . . .' he checked, and went on smoothly, '. . . or whether you don't. You would appear to be somewhat confused on the matter!'

She couldn't speak, a deep blush covering her features, as he continued to gaze down fixedly at her for a moment, before turning on his heel, scooping up his jacket and tie and leaving the room.

Left alone in the darkness, Annabel writhed in a torment of deep humiliation. Hugh had always been capable of making her intimately aware of her body's needs and desires, and he still possessed the talent to overwhelm any of the paltry defences she tried to erect against his fatal attraction.

She awoke the next morning feeling like death warmed up. She had a splitting headache and her eyes were still red and puffy from the bitter tears she had shed during the night. Moving sluggishly, she went to take a shower, which did nothing to lift her despondent spirits, as she trailed back into her bedroom and listlessly put on a dark blue dress whose elasticated bodice was held up with shoestring straps, over a full gathered skirt. A dark blue headband pulled her hair back severely from her face, and she was just putting on dark glasses to hide her swollen eyes when Tasmin came bounding in.

'Uncle wants to see us both—right away!'

Hugh was sitting behind his desk in the study, and smiled at Tasmin as they went in, while it seemed as if Annabel might not have existed, for all the notice he took of her.

'Tasmin,' he said, 'Helen Ford and her children are going off for the day on a fishing boat. They asked if you'd like to go too, and I said I thought you would. So off you go, and we'll see you later.'

'Oh, thank you, Uncle. Yo' is just a livin' doll!' she added in Josie's voice.

He laughed, and spanked her on the bottom. 'Off you go, imp!'

He swivelled around in his chair to watch her go across the garden, and then slowly swung back again. Annabel braced herself for what was to come. What did happen left her breathless and bemused.

Rising swiftly from his seat, Hugh grasped her hand and without a word led her from the room. Protesting weakly, she allowed herself to be towed upstairs to her room, where he left her by the door as he strode over to the large cupboard which housed her clothes. Throwing open the doors, he looked briefly through her few long dresses.

'Just as I thought,' he said in disgust. 'There's nothing here that isn't absolute rubbish!'

'What! How dare you . . .!' she nearly choked with sudden rage at his dismissive and contemptuous rejection of her clothes. 'Teachers don't have enough money to buy Paris models, you know!' she snapped bitterly, putting a weak hand to her throbbing brow.

'Precisely!' He turned and grinned suddenly at the trembling girl. 'Well, don't just stand there, Annabel. Come on, we haven't any time to lose,' he said firmly, as he ushered her from the room, and down the stairs. 'My car's outside. Go and sit in it, I won't be a minute.'

'Why in the hell should I? What's going on . . .'

'For God's sake, stop asking stupid questions and do as you're told!' he thundered. 'Now!' She took one look at his angry face, and bolted for the car.

Hugh, with Annabel beside him, drove to Bridgetown in silence. She didn't notice the lack of conversation, she was much too frightened, as he threw the supercharged Mercedes sports car around the many bends. His hands were tightly clenched on the wheel, as he drove like one possessed. She spent the journey with her eyes shut, clinging on to the seat and saying her prayers. The car slowed as they entered the busy streets of the capital, and Hugh found a parking space on the main street.

'Out you get,' he ordered, opening the door.

'Where are we going?'

'You'll see,' was his only reply

After about a hundred yards, he stopped at a boutique—Délice Modes—and opening the door shoved Annabel in before him. It was, clearly, a shop for those with a lot of money to spend. She noted that there were no price tickets on the clothes, and she knew that meant the dresses were very, very expensive.

As she looked around, she suddenly stood rigid with

shock and then walked slowly over to a medium-sized religious painting that hung on a far wall. She was studying it intently when a small whirlwind erupted through a curtain.

'*Ah, Hugh, chéri! Comment ça va?*' The whirlwind turned out to be a plump lady with grey hair in a bun on top of her head. Dressed in a simple black sheath dress, she gave Hugh a big hug and many kisses. 'Eet is so good to see you! Eet 'ave been so long!' The French accent was very pronounced.

'Come off it, Dora, you can relax—it's only me.' Hugh hugged her.

'But, Hugh—what about 'er?' pointing to Annabel.

'Oh, she doesn't matter.'

'How charming! Thank you very much!' Annabel glared at her employer.

'All right, Hugh,' the woman lapsed into a Cockney accent. 'Talking all that French rubbish is good for business, as you must have seen from the last set of accounts. I sell them French dresses from "Gay Paree" with a French accent—and everyone is happy—*n'est-ce pas?* Only I've got to speak like that all the time, or I'll slip up!' She smiled at Hugh and then frowned as she saw Annabel's interest in the painting.

''Ere! What do you think you're doing?' Annabel was lifting it down off the wall, to look at the back.

Oblivious to all else, Annabel looked at the picture, entranced. 'What's a genuine Correggio doing here?' she asked in tones of awe. 'The canvas is original . . . so are the stretchers . . . I don't believe it!'

'Right little clever dick, ain't yer?' said Dora, taking it from Annabel and putting it back on the wall. 'That, dearie, is my mascot—my little nest-egg. But if she can spot it, maybe I ought to put it in the bank?' she asked Hugh anxiously.

'Miss Wair is by way of being an expert in that particular field,' he reassured Dora.

Annabel was still looking at the canvas. 'Nest-egg? I should think it is! Do you have any idea what that would fetch in the London sale rooms . . .?'

'Well, this lovely man here gave it to me,' Dora gave Hugh a kiss. 'He gave it to me—for services rendered, you might say.'

'You might say,' agreed Hugh. 'Now to business, Dora. Rosalie Hunt is giving her annual ball. Of course, you must have sold most of the local worthies something to wear—right?'

'Right, dearie. Done very well, I have.'

'I want you to find something for this girl here, Dora.'

'What are you talking about . . .?' began Annabel.

'I promised Rosalie you would go to her ball, and go you will. She rang up early this morning to remind me—you're doing her flowers this afternoon, by the way—and I never break a promise.'

'Never break a promise? That's rich!' Annabel's face suddenly paled. 'I—I can't go to that dance. I mean . . .'

'Look,' said Hugh, 'let me put it bluntly. I personally couldn't care less what you do or don't want to do. Rosalie wants you to go to her ball—so you're going. Having said that, if you think I'm going to escort you there dressed in any of that rubbish in your cupboard, you've got another think coming!'

'I don't want to go the ball, and I certainly don't want to go with you—you ghastly man!' Annabel shouted. 'How dare you talk to me like that!'

'Very easily! And I can get worse. So shut up and do as you're told.' He turned to the woman. 'Dora, be a love and cart her off to see if you can find something that's suitable.'

Dora, who had been watching the lively exchange with interest, shrugged her shoulders, and pulled aside the curtain, beckoning for Annabel to go through.

Trembling with fury, Annabel went into the back of the shop. 'That bloody man! Who the hell does he think he is?' she yelled, hoping that Hugh could hear in the other room.

'That's men for you, ducks,' said Dora soothingly, as she went through the large racks of clothes, looking for a dress for Annabel.

'That man's not *for me*, I can assure you! Arrogant, stuck-up, opinionated, Victorian tyrant!'

'Yes, well, never mind,' Dora was still trying to pour oil on troubled waters. 'Here, love, slip into this.'

'The stupid man didn't tell me I was going to try a dress on,' explained Annabel, calming down a little, although still very angry. 'I'm not wearing a bra. Will it matter?'

'Not for this dress, it won't!' Dora laughed.

Annabel stood back moments later and surveyed herself in the long mirror. It was a lovely dress of the softest white silk pleated chiffon, which curved and draped itself sinuously around her figure in sculptured folds. She was reminded of Greek statues she had seen clothed in a similar manner . . . almost similar.

'Come on, love,' said Dora. 'We'll let the dog see the rabbit!'

Hugh stood rooted to the floor, with his mouth open.

'You may well look shocked!' Annabel was still very cross indeed, and misunderstood Hugh's expression. 'I don't know what the price is, but I do know that it's quite the *rudest* dress I've ever seen, let alone worn!' She looked down at the neckline which was open to the waist, displaying the fullness of her breasts each side of the exposed cleavage. A gold leather belt clasped the waist, before the skirt, open from the waist down, swept away to the ground.

'This, I'll have you know is a genuine Grès,' said Dora, crossly. 'No one, but no one can drape a material like she can.' She turned to Hugh. 'You want this girl to cause a sensation? Look!' She reached up, scooping Annabel's hair up in her hands, arranging it so it fell from a Grecian knot, down the nape of her neck.

Hugh groped for a chair, and sat down. He cleared his throat. 'Er . . . I see what you mean. We'll have it! Pack it up, Dora, and send me the bill.'

'Just a minute! We can end this little farce here and now,' snapped Annabel. 'You can't be seriously expecting me to wear this dress at Mrs Hunt's ball? I've never felt so naked in my life! I can just see it . . . one bend forward to pick up a drink, and I'm in a . . . a full-frontal situation, as the papers would say. No, thank you very much!'

'Now, see here,' said Dora. 'The designer of this dress is an artist with cloth, and a technician in design. Bend forward and see . . . you're quite safe. I know the skirt is split up the front, but it never opens too far, even if you sit down. Try it . . . there you are. All you have to do is to style your hair properly and—*et voilà!*'

'*Et voilà* nothing! This dress may be all you say, and I agree it's truly beautiful. On Sophia Loren, for instance, it would look perfect. But I'm Annabel Wair, governess, and I'll never be able to carry it off!' she wailed miserably.

What a dress! As she moved sideways, entranced with the shimmering folds of the material, she sighed regretfully, wishing she had the presence to wear such a glorious creation.

Hugh had clearly not been listening to a word she had said. 'Dora, you're an angel!' He turned to Annabel. 'Off you go and get back into your clothes.'

'Gladly! I've stood here exposing my all quite long enough!' She stalked back into the changing room with as much dignity as she could manage.

'She's got a point, you know,' said Dora as Annabel left. 'You'll have your work cut out keeping the men's hands off her!'

'Oh, I expect I'll manage.'

'Confident bastard, aren't you? I don't suppose dear Imogen will be any too pleased.' She gave a cackle of laughter. 'Funny, though,' she said, looking speculatively at the oil painting on the wall, 'fancy her knowing about something like that. You known her long?'

'About two and a half years,' he said, looking at her steadily.

'Oh Gawd!' she exclaimed, her eyes widening with comprehension. 'She's not the one who . . .?'

'Yes,' he interrupted curtly, before rising from the spindly chair with a deep sigh. 'She just turned up, out of the blue, to be Tasmin's new governess. I had no idea . . .' his voice trailed away, as he put a worried hand through his hair.

'Cripes, you're in a mess, aren't you?'

'"Cripes", my dear Dora, is hardly strong enough a word for the quagmire in which I find myself! You'd better go and give her a hand.'

Annabel was still fuming with rage, as she handed the dress to Dora. 'I'll never wear that dress—never! I'm sorry, I don't mean to be rude. It really is a fantastic creation, but he's only doing it to make fun of me. I ... I just can't take any more!' she cried, bursting into tears.

'There now, love,' said Dora, putting an arm around Annabel. 'There's no need to take on so. Come on, dry your tears.' She produced a lacy hanky from her cuff and gave it to the miserable girl. 'That's better. I don't know what this is all about, dearie, but I do know one thing, for sure!' and she held the dress in front of Annabel.

'Look at this dress—go on. Doesn't it look terrific, even on a hanger? If you saw it in a shop window, wouldn't you stop and stare at it longingly? Of course you would. Now, you have to believe me, you look simply sensational in it!' As Annabel, still sniffing, looked doubtful, Dora raised her hands in exasperation.

'There'll be some couturier dresses at the ball, of course. You'd expect the French contingent, for instance, to be well turned out. A couple of Diors and at least one St Laurent,' she mused to herself, 'possibly the Princess will wear a Balmain ... hm. However,' turning back to Annabel, 'I know the sort of guests Rosalie Hunt has invited—I should do, I've dressed most of them in my time. I give you my copper-bottomed guarantee that you, in this dress, will outshine all of them! What more could a girl ask, for heaven's sake! I know you think Hugh is making fun of you. I'm sure he isn't, but who cares? You're not going to be a joke—you, my dear, are going to be the belle of the ball!' With a crackle of laughter, Dora added, 'I feel quite like Cinderella's Fairy Godmother, I really do.'

'Are you really sure . . .?'

'Now, don't start all that nonsense again, love. I'm quite exhausted with all this drama. Put on your dark glasses, you don't want him to see you've been crying. I tell you what—I was asked to the ball by Rosalie, but I said "no". After all, at my age, who wants to dance until four in the morning? However, I'm definitely going now—I wouldn't miss it for worlds. How's that for a vote of confidence?'

Annabel hugged Dora. 'You've been so kind. I—I'll try and remember what you've said, but . . .'

'Come on, dear, let's have a touch of the stiff upper lip. Off you go, and don't worry.'

Back in the car, Annabel glanced swiftly sideways at Hugh as he concentrated on steering them through the crowded streets. Anyone seeing me in this glamorous car with such a handsome man would envy me, she thought miserably. How little they knew!

Hugh broke the oppressive silence that had been maintained since they had left Dora's shop. 'I'm meeting Brett at the Hilton to discuss some business, and I've arranged for him to take you on to Henry Earl's castle to do the flowers for Rosalie's ball tomorrow night.'

Annabel sat rigidly in her seat, staring straight ahead and ignoring Hugh's words. He gave a deep sigh. 'You looked very ... er ... really quite splendid in that dress. You really don't have to worry, you know,' he said in a warm, kind voice, turning to look at her, as he waited for the lights to change.

She hardened her heart against him, considerable effort though it was. What right had he to treat her and the only clothes she could afford as if she and they had crawled out of the woodwork? Pushing her around like some inanimate object, not to mention the way he had treated her last night! I—I could cheerfully kill him, she raged inwardly, as the car came to a stop outside the Hilton Hotel.

She jumped out of the car and slammed the door as she turned to face him. 'There's no need to be so damned condescending!' she hurled the words at him in fury.

'You look magnificent when you're angry, Annabel.' Hugh, still sitting in the car remained maddeningly calm.

'Don't you dare to patronise me, you—you arrogant

beast! You may be a lord, but you're certainly no gentleman!' she stormed.

'Now just a minute!' Hugh got out of the car and marched around the side of the vehicle, his face tightening as her insults struck home. They stood facing each other like fighting cocks, and were prepared to start trading insults when a lazy American voice interrupted, 'Is this a private fight, or can anyone join in?'

'Oh, Brett! I'm so glad to see you!' Annabel gave him a shaky smile, immensely relieved to see a friendly face, after such a morning fraught with tension.

'You can take it that we're both glad to see you,' Hugh smiled wryly. 'Let's have a cool drink and then we can all calm down.' He led them to the Terrace Café of the Hilton, which looked out over golden sands edged by the blue Caribbean Sea. After ordering Rum Punches the men got down to discussing some papers Brett had brought with him, while Annabel wandered over on to the terrace, looking at the sun-worshippers lying stretched out on wooden sun-beds.

She heard Brett call her name, and retracing her steps she found Hugh, business finished, ordering another round of drinks.

'Brett here is going to take you off now to do the flowers for Rosalie's ball. All right?' He looked at her steadily, with a small frown, which cleared when she nodded silently as she sipped her punch.

Hugh turned to Brett. 'Tasmin's off for a day on a boat, so there's no need for Annabel to hurry back . . .' he hesitated. 'Just . . . er . . . look after her, O.K.?'

'Sure thing, old buddy,' Brett grinned at his friend. 'I did get the message some time ago, you know!' he added cryptically.

Hugh looked at him steadily for a moment, then relaxed, smiling faintly at his old friend. 'Thanks,' he said simply.

'Have you two finished your business or haven't you?' Annabel asked crossly, dimly aware of some undercurrent between the two men which she didn't understand. 'Because if you haven't, I can always go and sit in the sun.'

'I think that we've clarified matters between us,' said Brett with a grin. 'Come on, honey, let's go and see Mom.'

Sitting now on the one comfortable sofa in a room otherwise full of delicate eighteenth-century French chairs, Annabel marvelled at the extraordinary house in which she found herself. It was called a castle, and she supposed that technically it was, as it stood four-square on rising ground, overlooking the Atlantic Ocean down below. Painted white and topped by battlements, on every side it had broad marble steps that led up to the wide verandah which encompassed the whole house.

She had followed Rosalie through room after room, full of valuable furniture and paintings. The large American woman might admit to being a magpie collector, but she certainly had an eye for quality. Lying here now, the scent from the bowls of pot-pourri mingling with the perfume on the warm breeze from the open french windows, Annabel found herself relaxing for almost the first time in days . . .

The next thing she knew was that a hand was softly shaking her shoulder, and she opened her eyes to see Rosalie bending anxiously over her.

'Oh, I'm sorry, Rosalie, I must have slipped off for a few minutes.'

'More like two hours, honey!' Rosalie laughed. 'I came in to find you sound asleep, and I reckoned that it was better than aspirin any day. How are you feeling now, dear?'

'Oh, I'm—I'm feeling fine. My headache's gone,

thank goodness,' she smiled at the older woman. 'I hope I haven't been a nuisance?'

'For heaven's sakes! A lovely girl like you, giving up her time to come and do some really fan-tas-tic flowers? Don't be silly, darling. I tell you what, how about you and me having a little drink?'

'When I've got rid of this ball,' said Rosalie as they sat in her private sitting-room upstairs, 'I'd be truly grateful if you would look over some of my little old paintings. I've got a very good agent,' she explained, 'but I have a feeling that just lately he's been charging me too much for some pictures. I sure hate to think that someone is taking me for a ride, honey!'

Annabel, carefully sipping a Manhattan that was strong enough to make her hair curl, explained that it was some three years since she had been involved in the art world. She tried to explain that prices could be very volatile, and that she was no expert.

'I'd still like your opinion,' Rosalie said stubbornly. 'Hugh tells me you're very good. Is that where you met him, in London?'

'Yes. He . . . er . . . brought in a picture. It was all a long time ago, though,' Annabel added hurriedly.

'His wife must have been still alive then. That poor dear man—my heart used to bleed for him, you know.' Rosalie shook her head sadly.

'I suppose he . . . he must have been shattered when . . . when she died.'

'Nonsense, darling—it was a merciful release for all concerned.' The brisk tone of Rosalie's voice surprised Annabel.

'Surely . . .? I mean . . . Was she very ill before she died?'

'Ill?' The American woman looked strangely at Annabel. 'Well, honey,' she drawled, 'I suppose injecting oneself with the Big H would make anyone ill!'

'The Big H ...?' Annabel looked at her in bewilderment.

'Heroin, darling—heroin. Hugh's wife was a dope addict. Surely you knew that?' she said, gazing with concern as the blood drained from Annabel's face and her large blue eyes widened with horror.

CHAPTER NINE

'I . . . I HAD no idea . . .' Annabel whispered, her mind in a daze. She shook her head, almost unable to comprehend Rosalie's words.

'I'm not surprised you didn't know,' the American woman was saying. 'The poor lamb tried to keep it all very quiet—for the sake of the family, I suppose. Brett and I were over for a visit and Hugh invited us to dinner one night. Well, I could tell right away that something was wrong. Hugh was like a cat on hot bricks, his wife wasn't to be seen—not that we'd met her before, of course.'

Rosalie explained that Brett had met Hugh in America, when Hugh was working on the New York Stock Exchange. 'The lovely man used to come and have brunch with us every Sunday : . .' She paused. 'Where was I?'

'The—the dinner party.'

'Oh yeah. Well, in comes Dora . . .'

'Dora? Not the woman who has the dress shop? No, it couldn't . . .'

'Oh, sure—that's Dora. She used to look after Hugh's wife—tried to keep her under some sort of control, I guess. Anyway, she came hurrying into the room looking distraught, Hugh and she disappeared and Brett and I were left to twiddle our thumbs on our own. It seemed years before Hugh came back, and it took us some time to persuade him to let his hair down—poor dear!'

'How awful!' breathed Annabel.

'I'll say! That poor man had been trying to keep her

150

away from her pusher, but she'd managed to get out and get herself a fix. Well, as you can imagine, the dinner party was all shot to hell, so Brett and I took him off for a meal at the Ritz. Hugh told us he'd forced her to take the cure he didn't know how many times, but she just didn't have enough guts to go through with it. I believe she was a lovely girl when they got married, but Brett, who saw her near the end, said she looked like an old woman. It's all a truly, truly sad story.'

'I didn't know . . . I had no idea . . . Why didn't he say anything to me?' Annabel's hands shook and trembled so much the ice clinked against the glass in her hands. 'If only he'd told me . . .' she whispered desperately, gazing at Rosalie, her large eyes deep blue pools of abject misery.

'Oh, honey!' the American woman hurried over to the distraught girl and folded her in her arms. 'Don't cry, darling. Me and my big mouth! It's all right, darling, hush now. You tell old Rosalie all about it, honey.'

Her head pillowed on Rosalie's huge bosom, Annabel poured forth the tangled story of the relationship between herself and Hugh. 'When I found out he was married,' she hiccuped through her falling tears, 'I l-left London to look after my m-mother who was ill, and . . . and afterwards I n-never w-ent b-back. No wonder,' she said sorrowfully, as she tried to wipe away her tears, 'no wonder he felt I'd betrayed *him*! But you see, all I could think about was how he had used *me*!'

'Still, you've found yourselves together, at last,' Rosalie said comfortingly.

'Oh no,' wailed Annabel. 'It's all awful now. He's got Imogen, and . . .'

'Land sakes alive, honey, he's never going to marry

Imogen! She's just . . . Well, you know what men are, darling. She was just . . . see here! You wouldn't expect him to shut himself away like a monk, would you?'

'It's not just Imogen, we fight and quarrel all the time. I'd have left long ago if it wasn't for Tasmin. She's such a lovely little girl,' Annabel said sadly, trying to hold back her tears.

'Do you love him? I mean, do you *really* love him?' Rosalie asked quietly.

Annabel nodded silently, wiping her eyes, and striving to regain control of herself. 'Yes,' she said softly, twisting her handkerchief between her hands, the long curtain of her blonde hair shielding her face. 'There'll never be anyone else for me,' she said simply, raising her unhappy eyes to Rosalie.

'How does he feel about you?'

'I . . . I don't know. He's so hard and cruel, sometimes. Really angry—for no reason. And then . . .' she shrugged. 'I really don't know,' she whispered.

'Why don't you tell him how you feel?'

'*Oh no*, I couldn't! There's Imogen, and . . . Oh no, I really couldn't!'

'Nothing happens on this island without my getting to hear about it. Right? So I can tell you that your Hugh hasn't seen Imogen—alone, that is—since the day you arrived out here. Believe me, honey, I know! Poor Hugh has been spending most evenings drinking alone at the Sandy Lane Hotel—that's a gen-u-ine fact!'

'How do you know that?'

'I always protect my sources,' Rosalie said in a deep stage voice, before reverting to her normal tones. 'Look, honey, you make quite an impression on my Brett, but he thought the set-up and the atmosphere wasn't quite right, O.K.? So he comes to his old mom and says, "What gives?" So, I do a little digging.'

'Oh, Rosalie!' Annabel smiled weakly at the older woman.

'So you can take it from me that poor Hugh has been trying to avoid dear Imogen as much as he can. But he's a nice guy. I mean, he's not likely to say to her, "Push off and get lost, baby, my true love has just arrived", now is he? You want to know what I think? I feel real sorry for the guy—that's what I think!'

'Yes . . . I hadn't thought . . .'

'Well, you do some thinking, honey. We're all so concerned with ourselves that we're apt to forget that other people have problems—huh? Just you remember that life's too short to be stuck with silly pride.'

After a light supper, Brett drove Annabel home through the gathering dusk of a warm Barbadian evening. She was very quiet, her mind full to overflowing with the information imparted by Rosalie. So abstracted with her thoughts was she, indeed, that she looked up startled to find that she had arrived back at the plantation house.

'I'll see you tomorrow night—you'll outshine them all, honey!' Brett gave her a friendly peck on the cheek, and watched until he saw her enter the house, before driving off into the night.

The house seemed to be deserted as she slowly, still deep in thought, wound her way upstairs to her room. Almost in a daze, she undressed and went to lie in a hot steamy bath, her mind still overwhelmed with what she had learnt that day.

Despite her mental exhaustion she found she couldn't sleep, as the self-accusatory and recriminatory thoughts chased themselves confusedly about her tired brain.

At last she gave up the struggle. Maybe, if she relaxed and read for a little while, sleep might come at last. Swinging her legs out of bed, she looked at her watch. It was one o'clock in the morning. There would be no one about if she went down to the library to try and find something to read.

Annabel tiptoed down the wide staircase, the only noise being the faint rustle of her thin silk nightgown as she moved across the hall and slowly opened the library door. She was surprised to find a lamp glowing dimly, as she went to the shelves to select a book. It was only as she turned to leave the room that she realised that she was not alone.

Hugh was lying stretched out on a leather-buttoned chesterfield, fast asleep. She moved slowly over to stand looking down at his long, lean figure, the lamplight casting deep shadows on his handsome face. Bending forward, she gently removed a small leather-bound book which was about to drop to the floor from his open fingers.

As she knelt beside him, Annabel's heart was wrung with love and sorrow, as she gazed tenderly down at the man who meant all the world to her. A lock of his curly hair had fallen over one of his heavy eyelids, and almost of its own volition, her hand moved slowly forward to smooth it back from his brow, her fingers slipping lovingly through the wiry black curls.

Her wrist was suddenly grasped by a firm hand, and she glanced quickly down to find Hugh's open eyes regarding her steadily, their expression unfathomable. Time seemed to stand still as they gazed at each other.

'Hugh, I . . .' Annabel's cheeks flushed under his intense scrutiny. 'Rosalie . . . she told me about . . . about your wife. Oh, Hugh . . .' her large blue eyes swam with tears, 'you should have told me . . .' She could proceed no further with her stumbled words, as Hugh's strong arms closed about her slim form, drawing her kneeling figure to him in a warm and tender embrace. His mouth covered hers in a kiss of such piercing sweetness that it was almost more than she could bear.

His hands moved caressingly over her trembling body, until with a deep groan, he leant forward and lifted her lightly, to lie beside him, moulding her slim frame to the hardening contours of his firm body. 'Bella ... Bella, my love,' the urgency in his low, husky voice, as he covered her face with light kisses, awoke an answering flame as shaking with desire she ardently responded to the demanding intensity of his mouth, as once more he possessed her lips.

'Dear God, how I want you!' he muttered hoarsely, looking down into her beautiful face, 'but not here— not now.'

'Oh, Hugh, I ...'

'Hush,' he gently smoothed the cloud of her long hair away from her face. 'You must go upstairs now,' his voice was thick, his breathing fast and unsteady, 'otherwise I can't guarantee not to do something we'll both regret. Come on,' he sat up, and then rose from the chesterfield, bending down to help her to her feet, holding her trembling figure which would have fallen without the support of his embrace.

'We'll talk later,' he whispered, once more claiming her lips in a swift kiss, before he firmly ushered her to the door.

Tasmin had begged to be allowed to be present while Annabel got ready for the ball at Henry Earl's castle. 'Please may I? Like I used to watch Mummy get dressed up in the evening?' she had begged. Annabel had felt a pang of sorrow for the little girl, who had lost her parents so tragically, and had willingly agreed; although as she tried to style her hair, she was beginning to regret it.

Tasmin, sitting on her bed, was chattering away nineteen to the dozen, and distracting Annabel in her difficult task of trying to arrange her hair in a Grecian style. 'Please, darling, do try and be quiet for a moment, I've got to a tricky bit, and I have to concentrate.'

Holding her tongue for five whole minutes was an obvious torture for Tasmin, but she managed it. 'There,' said Annabel, 'how's that?'

'It's fine, Annabel. You look really great!' Well, not too bad, anyway, Annabel thought, as she slipped out of her silk dressing gown and put on the dress. It was certainly easy to get into. All she had to do was to fasten the hooks at the waist and tie the gold belt. She turned to show Tasmin, who let out a wolf whistle.

'Really, Tasmin!' Annabel tried to look severe, but only succeeded in giggling as the child's eyes grew round in surprise.

'Wow! That's really a dress. Are you sure you won't fall out of it—if you know what I mean?'

'Yes, I know exactly what you mean, and no, I'm not entirely sure! However, I shall think positively and hope for the best. Can you see my shoes anywhere?'

Tasmin jumped off the bed to fetch the gold high-heeled strap sandals. 'It's a real shame, Annabel, that you and Uncle have to go to the ball with horrid old Imogen. It would be nice if we could wave a wand and make her disappear!'

'Tasmin, darling, I . . . I really can't discuss Miss Harrison with you. You know I can't. Furthermore, although I can't stop you thinking what you want to, you really must keep such thoughts to yourself.'

'Oh, sure—I know.' Tasmin sat cross-legged on the bed, deep in thought. Annabel was grateful for the ensuing silence, as she finished applying her lipstick with hands that trembled slightly. She was dreading the thought of the ball, and not only because she was having to wear such a revealing dress . . .

Her thoughts were interrupted by a knock at the door, followed by Hugh's voice asking if he could come in.

Glancing apprehensively at herself in the mirror, Annabel swallowed convulsively and braced herself. 'Yes, I'm . . . I'm ready,' she called as Tasmin ran to open the door. Or as ready as I ever will be, she thought in trepidation.

Her pulses raced at the sight of Hugh's tall, authoritative figure lounging in the doorway, noticing almost inconsequentially how well his white dinner jacket contrasted with his sombre colouring, and the way his hooded grey eyes widened as his gaze swept over the girl in front of him.

Unnerved by the lengthening silence, Annabel turned away to fiddle nervously with her things on the dressing table. Hugh had been busy about the estate, and she hadn't had an opportunity to talk to him since their meeting in the library last night. As the long hours of the day had dragged by, she had found herself becoming more and more apprehensive as wild optimism gave way to worried depression. Had he really called her 'my love', and . . . and had he meant it? How could he—especially when he and Imogen . . .

She started nervously, turning as Hugh cleared his throat. 'I . . . er . . . I come bearing gifts,' he said huskily. 'Actually, and to be precise, I'm carrying out Dora's instructions on the telephone this morning.'

He came forward, placing two small leather boxes on the round table in the middle of the room. 'Come here, Annabel,' he commanded, opening the small cases to display diamond stud ear-rings the size of large peas, and what looked like a diamond bracelet.

'Oh no!' she gasped. 'I can't . . . I really can't . . .'

'My dear Annabel,' he drawled, 'these belonged to my mother—I haven't stolen them! Besides, I'm a lot more frightened of what Dora would say if I refused to obey her orders than of your views on the matter. Do I make myself clear?'

His warm smile and the laughing gleam in his eyes removed the sting from his words, and with a timid nod of assent she moved slowly towards him, taking the ear-rings from their case. She was intensely aware of his nearness, the way his tall figure towered over her, as her trembling fingers fixed the diamonds on her earlobes.

'Now, I want you to stand still as this is going to be the tricky bit,' he said, opening the bracelet and fitting it over the large knot of hair at the back of her head. She shut her eyes for a moment, feeling faint as her heart began to pound at the close proximity of his body.

'I . . . er . . . I thought it sounded a bit mad, but Dora assured me that it would be perfect for your hair style. She . . . er . . . she was right.' His voice seemed to be oddly constrained, and she was unable to repress an involuntary shiver as his hands moved softly down her hair, his arms closing gently about her slim body.

'Tasmin . . .!' she breathed warningly, her eyes flying open to look feverishly around the room, desperately anxious to avoid meeting the gleaming grey eyes regarding her so . . . so disturbingly.

'The perfect governess!' Hugh murmured wryly, releasing her and stepping back. He looked around the empty room. 'Your pupil seems to have disappeared, Bella. However, you're quite right. What shocking behaviour, and in a lady's bedroom too!' he teased her, the gleam in his hooded eyes more pronounced than ever.

As if being in a lady's bedroom ever stopped your previous amorous activities! she thought, with a sharp sudden return of her old antagonism towards the tall, dark figure regarding her so intently.

'That dress, Bella, is quite . . . quite . . .' She looked up startled from her dismal thoughts at the hoarse, husky tone in Hugh's voice, and caught a glimpse of herself in the long mirror. Her hair was swept up in soft waves to the back of her head and clasped in a knot now covered in diamonds, continuing to fall in a golden stream down over her shoulders. The sleeveless white chiffon dress, bare of any ornament, swept and curved over her tanned body, while one slim leg was visible as the dress opened to fall away behind her. It was as if she was looking at some strange woman, not herself at all.

'Bella, you look absolutely . . . er . . . absolutely lovely. I . . .' He clenched his jaw, a pulse beating wildly in his temple as he suddenly checked himself and strode to the door. 'Dora also sent over a long white silk cloak. It's downstairs with the champagne. I think—in fact I know—I need a drink,' he said slowly, his face now a blank mask as he offered her his arm to lead her from the room.

Most of the servants had, somehow, managed to find necessary jobs in the hall, and as Hugh led her down the stairs there was an audible gasp as Annabel came into view.

'Lordy, Miz Annabel, yo' are a sight fo' sore eyes!' cried Josie, laughing happily at Annabel, who blushed a deep crimson at the praise, grateful to reach the sanctuary of the drawing room.

'We mustn't be too long,' said Hugh in a neutral voice, handing a glass to Annabel. 'I . . . I had arranged some time ago to . . . er . . . to take Imogen to the ball. We have to . . . to collect her on the way.'

'Yes, I know,' she replied quietly, burying her face in the rising bubbles of her champagne.

A few minutes of constrained silence followed, while Hugh studied one of the pictures on the wall, his hands thrust deep into the pockets of his slim black evening trousers. They were both relieved when Austin came into the room with a beaming smile for Annabel, before turning to Hugh.

'A telephone call for you, my lord. In the library,' he added.

Hugh returned a few minutes later. 'That was Imogen. Apparently she has arranged for someone else to take her to Rosalie's,' he said blandly, a small smile playing about his mouth as he poured himself another drink.

'I—I haven't said goodnight to Tasmin,' Annabel said hurriedly, finding her breathing suddenly difficult to control. 'I—I wonder where she is?' A moment later the little girl came in from the garden, a hand behind her back, her eyes gleaming with laughter.

'What have you been up to, imp?' Hugh demanded with a grin.

'I was only picking a flower for Annabel,' she said, producing a white lily from behind her back and gazing at her uncle with large grey, guileless eyes.

'Oh, darling, that's lovely! I hate to pin anything on this dress, so I'll just carry it with me.' Annabel bent down to give the child a kiss. 'You ought to go up and see Hannah now,' she added.

'Uncle Hugh said I could stay the night with the Ford's, didn't you, Uncle?' she begged. 'We're going to have a midnight feast and everything!'

'So I did,' he laughed. 'Off you go.'

Sitting silently in the car beside Hugh, Annabel clutched the white cloak tightly about her. She was dreading the prospect of the long evening which loomed ahead of her, fraught with difficulties. Imogen might have decided to arrive at the ball separately from Hugh, but there could be no doubt that once there, she would claim all his attention. Since Annabel was unlikely to know anyone at the castle, apart from Brett and Rosalie, she would almost certainly have to spend much of the evening watching Imogen and Hugh dancing together. Unhappy visions of the dark girl, tightly clasped in Hugh's arms, filled her mind with miserable despair.

Hugh turned to glance at her briefly, as a small sigh escaped her lips. 'Are you all right, Bella?' he asked softly in the darkness, before his attention was claimed by the twisting road ahead of him.

'Yes, I ... Yes, I'm fine,' she said as brightly as she could, a hard lump of depression settling down firmly in the pit of her stomach. Surely ... surely he would have said something after their encounter last night? He had promised that they would talk ... but they hadn't. If he cared for her ... really cared ... he would have found some time during the day ... sought some opportunity to speak to her. She didn't doubt Rosalie's story about his first wife. Poor Hugh! Her heart bled for the unhappiness he must have suffered, the torment he must have endured. But ... but that didn't necessarily mean that Rosalie was right about his present feelings for Imogen. It seemed far more likely that he was just waiting for Annabel to go back to England, before resuming his ... his relationship with the exquisitely lovely dark girl.

The heavy silence lengthened between them as she hunted desperately for something to say. Something—anything—to divert her unhappy and miserable thoughts. 'I—I forgot to ask Rosalie about ... about Henry Earl and his castle,' she said at last, annoyed

that her voice sounded too high and breathless. 'Can
... can you tell me about him?'

'Why not? It's a nice safe topic of conversation, isn't
it, Bella?' He gave a grim snort of sardonic laughter,
his hands tightening on the wheel, the taut hard lines
of his mouth and cheekbones thrown into sharp relief
by the headlamps of a passing car.

'Oh, Hugh, I ...' she looked at him helplessly,
laying a tentative hand on his arm in loving
compassion and confusion at the bitter note in his
voice. He took a hand off the wheel to catch her hastily
withdrawn fingers, raising them to his lips.

'I'm ... I'm sorry, my love,' he sighed softly, before
relinquishing her hand and relaxing in his seat. 'It's
not going to be my idea of a fun evening either, you
know.' His voice was gentle as he threw her a brief,
perceptive smile.

'I—I didn't ... I mean I ...'

'Henry Earl,' he said, firmly ignoring her stumbled
words, 'was a thoroughly bad man. He was born in the
late 1700s and came from an old Island family. He
sailed to England to marry a rich wife, and returned to
build his castle. He went through his wife's fortune
pretty smartly and treated her very badly, locking her
in his newly-built cellars until she managed to escape
and return to England. He had an absolute mania
about his castle, and apparently in pursuit of money to
complete his grand design, he took up wrecking. Not
at all a savoury chap, although Rosalie won't hear a
word against him.'

'Wrecking? Do you mean wrecking ships like they
used to do in Corwall?' she asked, interested in the
story despite her unhappiness.

'Yes. He'd tie lights to the trees down by the shore
and on the horns of his cattle, luring ships on to the
dangerous rocks below the castle. The poor sailors

thought they'd arrived at a safe harbour, and only found out the truth when it was too late. All Henry had to do was to wait for the tide to bring the cargoes ashore. A charming fellow! Here we are,' he added, as they swept down the drive and arrived outside the huge front door, which was brilliantly lit by liveried servants carrying flaming torches.

'I adore Rosalie,' he laughed, 'she never does anything by halves!' He got out of the car and came around to open her door. 'Don't worry, Bella. I'm sure . . .' His words were interrupted by the arrival of two other couples who greeted him warmly, as they passed through the massive double doors held open by yet more liveried flunkeys.

'Up you go, I'll wait down here for you.' Hugh gave her arm a comforting squeeze as she prepared to follow a servant up the sweeping marble staircase to a huge bedroom suite. Left alone, Annabel took a deep breath and removed her cloak, checking her make-up before nervously retracing her steps to the top of the staircase.

There could be no doubt that her entrance down the wide stairs caused a sensation. Hugh was talking to Rosalie and Brett, and it was Brett's involuntary cry of 'Wow!' that caused them all to turn and watch her descent.

Rosalie hurried forward. 'My gawd, you look absolutely rav-ish-ing! I can see you'll be the belle of the ball!' she cried, giving Annabel, who was trembling nervously, a big kiss. 'Just wait until you see the flowers this clever girl has done for me,' she said to Hugh. 'Everyone's raving about them!'

'Come on, let's go and dance,' said Hugh, putting a firm arm about Annabel's waist and leading her through the throng of brilliantly dressed and be-jewelled guests. She looked apprehensively around for

Imogen as Hugh stood hesitating for a moment on the edge of the dance floor, before bending down to whisper in her ear. 'I'm ... er ... a bit worried—it's rather public here. Will you promise to give me advance warning if you intend to slap my face again!'

Her startled eyes flew to his face, to find him grinning warmly down at her as he put his arms slowly about her slim figure. A blushing shamefaced gurgle of laughter was her only reply, but he obviously considered it satisfactory, as he gathered her melting body tightly in his embrace.

Time ceased to have any meaning for Annabel as she and Hugh moved to the music, oblivious to all else but each other, although she was surprised not to see Imogen among the guests. Her body swayed sinuously against his hard form, her heart beating faster than the slow tempo of the music, a burning flame of desire raging through her quivering figure.

Hugh seemed to be similarly affected. After a while he lifted his dark head from her cheek. 'I—I think,' he said huskily, 'we could both do with a cool drink.' Making their way towards the bar, they met Rosalie talking to a tall, dark-haired man with high cheekbones and hawk-like eyes.

'Hello, darlings,' trilled Rosalie. 'Meet my favourite Italian.' The stranger smiled as she performed the introductions, which Annabel missed owing to the noise of the other guests. The exceedingly handsome man bowed over her hand, and requested the pleasure of a dance. Hugh winked at her as she was led away by the stranger, to be swept around the floor in a waltz.

'Are you really in the Mafia?' she asked breathlessly, feeling dizzy as he steered her rapidly in and out of the other whirling dancers.

'How can you ask such a question? Do I look such a man? Is not possible!' he answered in a thick accent, smiling at her so wickedly that she very much feared it was entirely possible that Rosalie had described him accurately.

The music changed to a quickstep, whereupon Brett approached and tapped the man on the shoulder. 'Move over, you Italian dago! Stop monopolising this gorgeous girl!' The man laughed and relinquished Annabel, threatening to claim her again very soon.

'You look really superb,' Brett said with evident sincerity. 'Mom's right—you're going to be the belle of the ball! Are you having a good time?'

'Yes, wonderful!' she breathed happily, blushing to see Hugh standing against the wall with his arms folded, following her every move. 'That man I was dancing with—the man from the Mafia . . .'

'From the what?'

'Rosalie said he was from the Mafia.'

Brett threw back his head, and roared with laughter. 'Mom was only joking the other night at Hugh's dinner party. That's the Prince of Lombardy!'

'But I asked him if he was in the Mafia, and he didn't deny it.'

'Oh, boy! I'm going to enjoy pulling his leg about that. Come on, honey, I'd better take you back to Hugh. If looks could kill, I'd be lying in my coffin by now!'

'About time too, old buddy,' Hugh growled at Brett, before firmly taking hold of Annabel again. 'How about getting ourselves a drink, and then maybe you'd like a bite to eat?' He led the way into yet another room, which was less crowded. 'Ah, one of your flower arrangements, I see,' he said, placing a glass in her hands.

'The trouble is that they're Dutch pictures, and full of fruit as well as flowers,' she explained, walking over with him to examine her handiwork.

'They're beautiful,' he said admiringly. 'Really lovely. Are you enjoying yourself?' His eyes looked at her mockingly over his drink.

'Yes. I . . . I'm sorry I caused such a fuss in Dora's shop. It's just that . . .' she paused, confused by the gleam in his hooded eyes.

'Nothing seems to be—how shall I put it—out of place with that lovely dress,' he grinned as she looked down quickly, blushing a fiery red as she glanced up to meet the mocking glint in his eye, the amused twist of his sensual mouth. 'Come on, Annabel, relax! Let's go and find some supper.'

They were just about to go into the dining room when Brett hurried up, a worried look on his face. 'You'd better come quickly, Hugh. There's a bit of trouble, I'm afraid. I wouldn't bother to bring Annabel . . .'

'Nonsense. I'm certainly not letting you and that Italian get your hands on her again!'

Annabel didn't think there was anything like that on Brett's mind, as he shrugged and led them quickly through to the hall, a worried frown on his face. Hugh was still firmly clasping her hand as they arrived at the bottom of the great marble staircase to find Imogen, her face dark with fury, complaining in a loud angry voice to Rosalie, who looked a little ruffled.

'There she is!' Imogen shrieked as they came into view. 'There's that dreadful girl! Just let me get my hands on her, that's all!'

Annabel looked at her with startled bewilderment, as Brett attempted to calm the other girl down, suggesting that they adjourn to the study to sort out the trouble, whatever it was.

'There's nothing to sort out!' Imogen shouted in fury, as she nevertheless allowed herself to be shepherded into a small room off the hall. 'The way she's behaved! The nasty, sneaking . . .'

'That's quite enough!' Hugh's voice cut like a whiplash across her angry words. 'Kindly explain what's wrong, in a quieter tone, and stop making an exhibition of yourself!' He looked at Imogen with contempt, as he slowly opened his gold case and casually lit a cigarette.

Imogen ground her teeth with rage. 'That—that ghastly girl rang me up, just as I'd finished dressing for the ball, to say that you'd be half an hour late in picking me up. I waited . . . and waited . . . and in the end I phoned your house. Austin was very rude—you should sack him immediately! I had to go to all the trouble of getting a taxi . . . I couldn't get hold of one for ages!' Her voice rose higher, as she turned viciously on Annabel.

'You'd do anything to get your claws into him— wouldn't you?' she screamed, completely losing control. 'My God! Look at you—dressed like a tart! I've watched you—little Miss Prim and Proper— "Yes, my lord", and "No, my lord"— now you can see what she's like, Hugh!'

Annabel blanched and leant trembling against the wall, as the vicious words flowed over her. She looked uncomprehendingly at Hugh, who continued to smoke, as she tried to make some sort of sense out of what Imogen was saying.

'If you've quite finished . . .?' Hugh's curt voice halted the flow of vindictive malice and in the small silence that followed, Annabel found her voice.

'I—I never telephoned you. I—I couldn't have. I was upstairs getting dressed . . . and then Hugh came in. I promise you, I never went near a telephone,' she protested anxiously.

'Of course she didn't—I can vouch for that,' Hugh said firmly. 'In fact we can stop this stupid farrago of nonsense right now. It was you, Imogen, who telephoned me just as we were about to leave, and told me quite clearly that you'd arranged a lift with someone else. Why you should feel it necessary to concoct this extraordinary tissue of outrageous lies, I have no idea. I suggest you apologise to Annabel immediately!'

Imogen took one look at his contemptuous face and completely lost her head. 'You're lying!' she shrieked, stamping her foot and trembling with rage. 'You're every bit as bad as that ghastly so-called "governess". A teacher for Tasmin . . .!' she laughed wildly. 'That's a laugh! Why, she's nothing better than a little bit of built-in home comfort! Just look at her—standing there practically naked . . .'

'Be quiet!' Hugh thundered.

'No, I won't!' she yelled, her lovely features twisted into a mask of fury, as she ran forward and struck him hard across the face.

'Hold it, girl!' Brett stepped forward and caught her arm as she raised it to hit Hugh's rigidly still figure once more.

'I—I was with Hugh when you telephoned,' Annabel's quiet words dropped like stones into the pool of silence that had followed Imogen's outburst, 'so I can support everything he says. It's not . . . not Hugh who's lying.' Still quivering nervously from the verbal assault and the storm which had burst about her head, she looked with concern at Hugh's face, white with outrage, except for the red mark of Imogen's hand. His eyes were blazing with fury, and it was evident that he was controlling himself with great difficulty.

He strode to the door and opened it. 'Annabel would like some supper, Brett. I'd be grateful if you would look after her. Miss Harrison and I have a few things to say to each other—in private, if you please.'

'Sure thing.' Brett took Annabel's arm and led her shaking figure from the study.' Come on, honey,' he said reassuringly as she looked back anxiously at the closed door. 'It's better if you make yourself scarce for a while. Hugh wouldn't like either of us to hear what he's going to say to Imogen—or vice versa, for that matter.'

'I don't understand it at all. I really didn't telephone her, you know. I mean, I don't even know where she lives or—or anything. There must be hundreds of Harrisons in the telephone directory—only I can't prove it,' she added unhappily.

'Of course you didn't, honey. You're just not the sort of girl who would do something like that. It would be stupid and childish, wouldn't it? Come on, let's have something to eat.'

'Something to eat' turned out to be a buffet supper that far exceeded anything Annabel could have imagined. Scores of liveried servants stood behind white linen-covered tables laid out all around the sides of the vast dining room, ready to serve the guests from dishes piled high with the most delicious food Annabel had ever seen. The centrepiece of all this magnificence was a three-foot-high flying fish, as if in flight from the sea, and she gave a gasp of wonder as she realised it was carved from a block of ice.

'I've never seen anything like this before in my life,' she said, still shaking nervously from the scene in the study, when someone called, beckoning from across the room.

'Over 'ere, *ma chère!*' called Dora, looking very elegant in a wine-coloured dress. Brett and Annabel were introduced to her companions, and Dora, French accent to the fore, complimented Annabel on her turnout. 'Are you enjoying yourself, Cinderella?'

'*Oui, certainement,* fairy godmother! *Et vous,*

madame?' she teased lightly, still trying to stop her hands from shaking.

'That's quite enough of that,' Dora interrupted hastily. She looked Annabel up and down. 'You look very beautiful, I must say. You do me credit!'

'I owe you a great deal,' Annabel agreed, sitting down with Brett at Dora's table, and trying not to think about what was likely to be going on in the study.

'Where's Hugh?' Dora asked Brett, who replied with a grim laugh, 'Having a few words with his ex-girl-friend, I imagine,' he said dryly.

'Like that, is it?' Dora smiled at him. 'Not before time,' she added sagaciously, winking at him over her glass of champagne.

'What I don't understand is who telephoned Hugh,' Annabel whispered to Brett. 'I really was there when he took the call. We were expecting to pick Imogen up, and she phoned just as we were about to leave.'

'She's just gone mad and completely lost her marbles, honey. What else? I mean, he must know her voice—who else could it possibly have been?'

Annabel stiffened, her fork poised in mid-air, as a dreadful thought suddenly occurred to her. It couldn't . . .? Surely not . . .? She tried to cast her mind back to the plantation house. It was! It must have been Tasmin who had made those phone calls. She didn't know how the child had done it, but she knew instinctively that the little girl had engineered the whole thing.

'I—I think I know who did it,' she burst out to Brett, as Dora looked at her in surprise. 'I must . . . I must tell Hugh and Imogen . . .'

'Too late, honey.' Brett nodded towards Hugh's advancing figure as he strode towards them, his tanned features cast into a hard, stern expression.

'It's been a lovely party, Brett,' he said blandly, 'but I'm sure you'll excuse Annabel and myself—under the circumstances.'

'Hugh! I've worked out what happened . . .'

'Yes, I know,' he gave her arm a warning squeeze. 'We'll just find Rosalie and say goodbye. Come along.'

He led her down the marble steps and into the car in silence. As he drove them home, she turned to look at his harsh features with trepidation. 'It's all my fault,' she said, miserably conscious of the fact that Tasmin was under her charge and in her care.

'Don't be silly, Bella. I know exactly whose fault it is!'

'Please don't be angry with Tasmin,' she pleaded.

'I'm not angry with anyone,' he said quietly, and didn't speak any more until they reached home.

As he escorted her across the hall and up the stairs in silence, Hugh's tall figure and stern features presented a forbidding aspect. Annabel, glancing through her eyelashes at his strained face, couldn't prevent a small shiver of apprehension from running down her backbone. Her tired mind seemed unable to cope with the dramatic ramifications of the evening, and it was with a sigh of relief she turned at her bedroom door to say goodnight.

'Hugh, I . . .'

'Are you about to thank me for a delightful evening?' His voice was heavy with irony, an eyebrow lifted in sardonic amusement.

'Well, I—I'm very tired. I think I'll just say goodnight . . .'

'Oh no, you won't!' He gave a dry bark of laughter, ignoring her startled cry of protest as he swept her up in his arms and strode down the corridor, kicking open the door of his bedroom and placing her firmly on his large, wide bed.

Shocked into silence, her eyes wide with apprehension and fright, she watched him retrace his steps to the door, the sound of the large key turning in the old-fashioned lock providing a resonant and determined note of finality in the silent room.

CHAPTER TEN

LOOKING at the stern, unrelenting expression on Hugh's tanned face, Annabel's wide, apprehensive eyes looked about her in panic. There seemed no escape from the tall dark figure leaning nonchalantly against the locked door, and she could read nothing in the hooded grey eyes regarding her so intently.

'Please, Hugh—this is ridiculous! I must go.' Her voice was breathless and unsteady, as she sat up and swung her legs off the bed.

'You're not going anywhere.' The quiet finality of his tone was far more frightening than any angry words could have been, and she felt her limbs beginning to tremble in an alarming manner.

'You can't possibly keep me here,' she said as lightly as she could, the slight wobble in her voice betraying her inner turmoil, as she rose and took a step towards him.

'Can't I?' he said blandly, moving towards her, his tread as lithe as a panther. Confused by the glint in his determined eyes, she backed away from him, so that it only required a gentle push from his hand to send her sprawling back on to the bed.

Ignoring her flustered and dishevelled figure, he turned away to shrug off his white evening jacket. 'The last two weeks have been almost the most exhausting of my life,' he said sternly, his hands moving up to undo his black bow tie. He leant against a chest of drawers, his hard fierce eyes pinning her to the bed as effectively as if they had been made of steel.

'I am simply not prepared to put up with any more

173

nonsense—from you or from anyone else,' he continued, slowly removing his gold cufflinks. 'I said last night that we would have a talk, and so we will. Not a long one,' his mouth twitched in silent humour, 'but a talk, nevertheless. By that I mean that I'm going to talk, and you're going to listen. Do I make myself clear?'

Annabel nodded silently, unable to say anything. There seemed to be a large obstruction in her throat, she felt slightly sick and her heart was pounding so loudly that she felt certain he must be able to hear it.

'Lost for words? That makes a change!' His eyes gleamed with cynical amusement as he slowly unbuttoned his shirt. 'As I said, the drama of the last two weeks has been exhausting, and I, quite frankly, have had it! You and I, my darling Bella, are going to sort out our relationship right now, once and for all. Understand?'

A shiver ran through the length of her body as she stared mesmerised at his tall, lounging figure, the dark hairs on his deeply tanned chest now clearly displayed by his open shirt.

'Still silent? Remarkable!' He gave a dry bark of laughter, and removing the slim gold case from his pocket, lit a cigarette. He looked completely at his ease, his movements relaxed and unhurried as he slowly exhaled the smoke, his hard eyes still regarding her intently.

The blood raced through her body, pounding in her veins, as the silence lengthened between them, the air heavy with tension as her bones seemed to melt beneath his unwavering gaze.

'You know very well, my darling one,' he said at last, 'that I was madly in love with you two years ago. Deep in your heart, you also know that I'm far from being a "debauched libertine"—or indeed any of the epithets you've been casting my way these last few days. In fact, my delightful idiot,' he smiled grimly, 'you must be blind, deaf and dumb not to realise that I love you—*and only you*—to distraction!'

'Hugh, I . . .' she gasped breathlessly, as her heart seemed to lurch and turn over.

Hugh stubbed out his cigarette and walked slowly over to the bed, his eyes firmly fixed on Annabel's lovely, trembling figure. 'I've had a very long, and as its turned out, an emotionally fraught day. The only thing—absolutely the only thing—that's enabled me to retain even a vestige of sanity, my dearest love, has been the thought of making love to you!'

She shivered violently as he sat down beside her on the bed, unable to tear her eyes away from his wide sensual mouth, his gaze now warm and tender. 'The only point of discussion, therefore, would seem to be the state of your feelings regarding myself. Well?' he added sternly, as she nervously flicked her tongue over her dry lips.

'Tell me!' he commanded harshly, grasping her chin firmly and tilting her face up towards his own.

'You . . . You know I love you . . .' she admitted in a breathless whisper, so low and tremulous that he had to bend his dark head to catch her words. 'I—I've never been able to stop loving you, however hard I tried.'

'Oh, Bella—*at last!*' he groaned gently, slowly undoing the clasp of her dress and feasting his eyes on the soft warm body quivering beneath his touch.

'Oh no . . . please, Hugh, I . . .'

'Oh yes! Oh yes, my love,' his voice was husky and thick with passion as he ignored her whispered plea and brought his dark handsome face down towards her. His mouth closed over her lips in possessive hunger, gradually becoming soft and warm, so disruptively and erotically sensual that she felt faint with rapture.

Drowning in ecstasy, she surrendered to the flame that seered through her fevered body, as, gently removing her dress, he traced its disappearing path with scorchingly arousing intensity with his burning mouth. Annabel moaned helplessly beneath the light touch of his hands, ripples of almost unbearable excitement dancing across her skin as he gently stroked her trembling figure.

'So lovely . . .' he breathed, his mouth moving slowly down her arched neck, inexorably towards his hands, now gently insistently caressing her full, creamy breasts, whose rosy peaks were taut and swollen with desire. As his lips closed over a tender bud, she cried out at the shaft of almost painful emotion that exploded deep inside her.

He raised his head to look down at her, as she ran her fingers through the curly black hairs on his chest. 'Oh God, Bella, how I love you!' he groaned, his body shaking at her touch. Swiftly divesting himself of the rest of his clothing, he clasped her warm naked form tightly to him in a passionate embrace, once more claiming her lips in a hard, possessive kiss, before laying her gently down on the cool linen sheet.

With a wordless murmur of entreaty she lifted her arms, pulling him urgently down towards her soft, trembling body, overcome by the driving force of her love and need for him.

His lovemaking became more urgent, more arousing, as his hands and mouth moved erotically over her body, deep husky murmurs of endearments being torn from his throat as he trembled at her uninhibited and sensual response to his touch.

Panting for release from the tension which seemed to fill her whole existence, it wasn't until she was nearly swooning with desire, almost unconscious with delight, that his hard firm body covered hers, and he allowed his own hungry passion to have free rein. Annabel cried out with joy, great shudders shaking her slim figure as he brought them both to the very peak of sexual fulfilment, in an overwhelming explosion of mutual love and passion.

Annabel woke to find herself locked in Hugh's arms. She looked with bewilderment around the room lit by the early morning sun, her dazed and sleepy eyes realising that she was not in her own bedroom. Suddenly, with a rush, she remembered all that had happened the previous night. Blushing deeply, she looked down at her naked figure beneath the crumpled sheet, as she recalled how once more in the night, Hugh's light but insistent touch had aroused her, and how ardently and wantonly she had responded.

As memories of their passionate night together flooded her mind, she moved involuntarily and sensually against him, the motion of her warm body causing his eyes to flick open into wakefulness. He lay looking tenderly down at the lovely girl in his arms, before raising himself on one elbow, gently brushing the tangled mane of blonde hair away from her brow.

She flushed beneath his warm, loving scrutiny, protesting as he slowly peeled away the sheet covering her body. 'Hugh . . . no!' she said breathlessly, as his hand began to move lazily and caressingly over her soft skin. 'I—I must go back to my room. I . . . Tasmin . . . The servants!'

'Tasmin is staying with the Fords and the servants have all been given the day off. It's Sunday, after all, my love!' he said, his eyes gleaming with laughter, as he bent forward to possess her soft, red lips.

'You—you planned it all! Didn't you?' she gasped between his ardent kisses.

'Of course,' he answered simply, trailing his fingers slowly over her body.

'But it's wrong ... you can't ...' she moaned helplessly, as his hands became more erotic, more arousing.

His eyes darkened with desire. 'Is that a challenge?' he murmured, covering her with his hard, firm body.

'No, Hugh! Please, no ...' she whispered desperately, as she felt herself responding wantonly to his sensual touch.

'My dearest, darling Bella,' he drawled softly, dropping featherlight kisses on her upturned face. 'You must—you really must—learn to start saying "Yes, Hugh".' He smiled lovingly down at her. 'I really can't bear the thought of going through what I hope will be many years of married bliss, with you saying "No" to me all the time. It would be far too exhausting!'

'You—you want to marry me?' She lay trembling in his arms, tears welling in her large blue eyes.

'Ah, my dearest, please don't cry! I love you so much, my lovely Bella. I—I can't bear the thought of losing you again. Please say you'll marry me?' he pleaded anxiously, the love in his warm grey eyes making her heart leap and turn over.

'Oh yes,' she breathed, wiping away the tears of joy, 'I—I love you with all my heart. I always have.'

'I suddenly feel quite exhausted!' he laughed, rolling over on to his back. 'We must be married very soon, I really don't think that I can stand another two weeks of courtship—not like the ones I've just gone through!'

'*Courtship?*' She sat up, looking at him sternly. 'What courtship? You've been simply horrid to me—

you know you have! Are you sure you want to marry me?' she asked anxiously, suddenly assailed by doubts that somehow it could all be a dream.

'For God's sake! Of course I do, you wretched girl! I tried to propose once before, the night you went out to dinner with Brett, and all I got for my pains was a slapped face! Oh, darling, I—I made such a hash of it, didn't I? I couldn't seem to find the right words somehow.' He pulled her roughly to him, covering her face with fierce, possessive kisses.

'I—I thought you had . . . had someone else in mind,' she said breathlessly.

'I know,' he groaned. 'I managed to work it out as I was driving home that night. I was in such a state,' he laughed wryly. 'I could cheerfully have murdered Brett—not to mention strangling poor Imogen. Oh, darling, I've been in such torment, you've no idea!'

'Oh yes, I have,' she sighed, 'because I've been more miserable than at any time in my whole life. Well, since I found out you were married, that is.'

Hugh was silent for some time, cradling her within the safety of his arms. 'I don't know if you can understand,' he said at last, his voice low and strained, 'just what happened when I first met you. For about a year before that it had seemed as if I'd been in the midst of a living hell with my wife, and then—quite simply and violently—I fell in love, totally and irrevocably in love with a shy girl, with long ash-blonde hair and the bluest, bluest eyes I'd ever seen. You were so lovely and innocent. After the ghastly life with Venetia, your purity and innocence was like water to a man dying of thirst. Oh, my love,' he cried, holding her close to him, 'you must understand. Your love was all I had. I knew I'd lose you if you found out I was married.'

'Surely if you'd told me . . .'

'I—I couldn't take the risk, my dearest. You were the only point of sanity in my terrible world.'

'Was it so very awful?' she asked softly.

'Oh, Bella! You've no conception of how it was,' he groaned. 'Venetia had been such a lovely girl. I met her at a dance. She was only twenty, and she absolutely bowled me over. I wouldn't listen to anyone's advice—not I!' He gave her a crooked, painful smile. 'My older sister and my aunt tried to warn me, not because of the drug scene—they and I knew nothing about that—but because she was apparently very wild and had been very much indulged as her father's only child.'

He paused, before going on. 'I was, frankly, besotted and insisted that we got married as soon as possible. We went to Greece for our honeymoon, and . . . and I'll never forget the shock when I went into the bathroom unexpectedly and found her injecting herself. After she'd had her fix I shook the truth out of her. Apparently she'd been experimenting with hash and amphetamines for about a year, and had only just started on heroin when we married. I—I wasn't able to touch her, once I'd found out. I cut short the honeymoon and took her back to London to try and cure her of the addiction—all to no avail.'

'Oh, my darling, please don't distress yourself,' Annabel cried, throwing her arms about his unhappy figure.

'It's all right, my love. It all happened so long ago. It's just the damned horror of what the drug can do that has always appalled me—that and the men who push these drugs on unsuspecting, weak people. She was completely in the thrall of her pusher, and she had even *entertained* some of his friends in return for the drug, as I found out later.'

Annabel rocked him in her arms, as she would a

child. 'Oh, Hugh, it's so terrible! That poor girl, and you . . .' She couldn't continue, her voice was so choked with emotion.

He sighed deeply. 'I tried, she tried, we all tried to cure her. Nothing seemed to work, and at last I hired a companion for her. Someone to guard her, make sure the pusher didn't appear on the scene, and generally act as a kind wardress. Without Dora I would have lost my mind. There's *never* going to be enough I can do for her.'

'But Dora has a dress shop—I don't understand?'

'Dora had been a seamstress at a top London couturier's, but arthritis affected her hands. Not too badly, but it prevented her from doing the fine sewing at which she excelled. She replied to my advertisement, and I ever afterwards blessed the day she arrived. My life, from being a living hell, became bearable—just.'

He turned an anguished face to her. 'And then I met you. That summer was the most wonderful, and at the same time, the most terrible period of my entire life. There I was, madly in love with you, while at home there was Venetia. By now she looked like an old woman, thin as a rake, with eyes that burned in their sockets.' He shuddered at the recollection. 'All she lived for was the next fix. I'd registered her as an addict by then, in order to try and keep the pusher away. It was ghastly . . .' his voice died away. 'I—I wanted you so much. I tried to control myself, I really did, but your sweetness tormented my dreams, my every waking thought. It—it wasn't lust—I loved you, Bella, with my complete being, my mind as well as my body. In the end, of course, I—I couldn't contain myself, and—and we had three glorious days together.' He kissed her gently. 'It was so wonderful, but I knew how wrong it was to deceive you. I couldn't leave Venetia, I was all she had, and she was so ill by that time.'

'Oh, Hugh, if only you'd told me! I'm sure I'd have understood.'

'You're probably right, darling, but I was in such a panic at the thought of losing you that I don't think I was seeing straight by then. What cruel tricks fate can play!' he sighed deeply, his arms tightening about her. 'No sooner had I tasted heaven than I found myself in a far more hellish situation than I could ever have imagined! When your friend told me you never wanted to see me again, I was like a man demented. I combed London for a week looking for you, and then went on a drinking session to end all drinking sessions. When I sobered up and went back to the auction house, your friend had left for another job, and they wouldn't or couldn't tell me where you were. Dora was wonderful. I'd have slit my throat without her comforting shoulder to cry on.'

'Dora knows? She knows about me?'

'Yes,' he laughed softly. 'When I told her who you were—after we'd chosen that gorgeous dress—well, if I hadn't been so unhappy that day, I'd have laughed at her expression! I know, my love, that you thought I was being unkind about your clothes, but I knew you'd need something really special for that ball—and Dora produced it. When you came out of the changing room, my dearest Bella,' he laughed, 'I had to sit down, I was so thunderstruck. I'd never seen anything so sexy in all my life!'

'Oh, Hugh . . .' she protested laughingly, blushing as she kissed him gently on his ear, and there was silence for a while, only interrupted by softly whispered endearments. 'For heaven's sake, Hugh!' she gasped, lying back breathlessly, as he gazed lovingly down at her, 'you're quite . . . quite shameless!'

'I know,' he beamed. 'Shocking, isn't it! I'm looking

forward to you teaching me how to behave—although I hope you won't hurry your tuition, my little governess!'

His words reminded her of the reason for her arrival in Barbados. 'How did you come to live out here?' she asked, trailing her fingers over his long brown body.

'I can't possibly concentrate if you do that!' he laughed, removing her hand, and raising it to his lips. 'Oh, Bella,' he sighed, 'life is ironic, isn't it? Just one month after you vanished, Venetia evaded Dora one day, and managed to find someone to give her a fix. It turned out that the needle was dirty, and she got blood poisoning. She had no resistance and went into a coma, and died.' He sighed again. 'Poor Venetia, what a tragic life she had. My uncle died soon afterwards, and I escaped out here, for peace and sanctuary. I brought Dora out, and set her up in the shop, while I began to live the life of a plantation owner.'

'And then I arrived . . .' Annabel said slowly.

'My God! I've never had such a shock in my life as when I saw you standing in the drawing room that day. When my poor sister Caroline and her husband were killed, and I had Tasmin to look after, I expected some sort of middle-aged teacher to arrive. Never in a million years could I have imagined I would find my lost love.'

'And I,' she said, suddenly breaking into laughter, 'I was expecting to see an old man! I nearly fainted when you came into the room. You were so fierce and angry.'

'Well, wouldn't you have been?' Hugh brushed a hand through his curly hair. 'No, I don't suppose you would,' he smiled down loving at her. 'Darling, I was swept with a mixture of feelings,' he tried to explain. 'First there was rage at your having run away and left me. Then joy at seeing you again, only I was too stupidly proud to let you know how I felt. Finally, I was deeply depressed at your reaction to me—mostly one of fright and disgust.'

Annabel hung her head in shame. He was right, they had both had such mixed emotions, and had been at such cross-purposes with each other, for so long.

Hugh interrupted her thoughts. 'I had to try and keep you in the house, until matters straightened themselves out.' He smiled wryly. 'And before you accuse me of not even trying to engage a new governess—I'll plead guilty straight away.'

'I'm so glad you didn't try and get someone else,' she admitted with a loving smile.

'Oh, darling, it was such a mess. I couldn't make out what you felt for me. One moment you'd be spitting like a cat—all claws and calling me "my lord", and the next moment you would melt in my arms so lovingly . . . Oh, darling, I was absolutely bewildered. All I could cling to was the sure knowledge of how much I loved you.'

'Dear Imogen didn't help,' she said softly, looking down, not able to meet his eyes.

'Well, actually, she did. You were quite clearly jealous of her—and that gave me hope.'

'I wasn't!' she protested, with a blush. 'I wasn't at all jealous.'

'Oh yes, you were!' He laughed happily, clasping her waist, and rolling over on his back to look up at her flushed face and sparkling blue eyes. 'Come on—confess! My sweet, lovely and adorable liar.'

'Male chauvinist pig,' she muttered, with a grin. 'Oh, all right. I was jealous—just a little bit . . .' She couldn't say any more as he clasped her soft body firmly to him, covering her sweetly curved lips with a possessive kiss.

He rolled her over and lay looking down at her

seriously. 'I—I suppose if I'm to tell the truth, I . . . er
. . . I've behaved very badly to Imogen. I never had
any intention of marrying her, of course, but . . .' he
paused. 'I thought I'd lost you for ever,' he said
slowly, in a low voice. 'It doesn't excuse my
behaviour, of course.' He shrugged unhappily.

'Well, I can see she's very sexy.'

Hugh's face flushed with embarrassment. 'Do you
forgive me?' he asked.

'Of course I do—there's nothing to forgive,' she
reassured him lovingly. 'Just as long as your . . . er . . .
friendship with Imogen doesn't continue.'

'Bella!' he cried in horror. 'How can you think . . .?'
Her body shook with laughter, and he subsided
against the pillows with a groan. 'You wretch! I'm
going to have a terrible life—I see it all now—leg-
shackled for the rest of my days to a nagging wife!
Mind you,' he added seriously, 'I will have to see
Imogen once more, I'm afraid.'

'Why? Oh yes, I see . . .' she said slowly, as
comprehension dawned.

'I may have a lot to thank Tasmin for, nevertheless
she can't be allowed to get away with what she did. I
shall have to take her to see Imogen, and make the
child apologise. That will be sufficient punishment, I
think.'

'What I don't see,' said Annabel as his warm arms
closed about her once more, 'is how she did it?
Imitating Imogen's voice and mine would be no
problem to her—she's a brilliant mimic. But how did
she physically manage the telephone calls?'

'I realised even before you and Brett left the room
last night that Tasmin's little Machiavellian hand lay
behind the apparent muddle. While Imogen was
ranting and raving, I was trying to work it out. I'm
almost sure Tasmin must have slipped out to George

Ford's office in the stable block. There's a telephone there and it has a different number from that in the house.'

'Of course!' Annabel exclaimed. 'She came in from the garden after you'd talked to Imogen ... or who you thought was Imogen.'

'If I hadn't been so—so preoccupied with you, my love, I might possibly have noticed something amiss. As it was, all I could think about was how soon I could manage to get my hands on your lovely body.'

'Hugh! Really!'

'.... and I was so delighted to be relieved of Imogen's company,' he continued, disregarding her laughing protest with a sardonic smile, 'that I just put down the phone with a grateful sigh of relief.'

'Was—was the row in the study really awful?' she asked, her eyes shadowed with concern.

'Not too good. Of course,' he frowned unhappily, 'as soon as I realised it was all Tasmin's fault, I tried to calm Imogen down. Unfortunately, she'd gone way past the point where she was capable of listening to reason. I—I think I'd like to draw a veil over the whole episode, darling, if you don't mind.'

'Oh, Hugh—poor Imogen! I do feel sorry for her. Especially now that I'm so happy,' She lovingly kissed his ear. 'How did Tasmin manage the earlier call? The one where she pretended to be me?'

Hugh laughed. 'She must have phoned Imogen from the telephone in the library when I was fixing that necklace over your hair. Where is it, by the way?'

'Oh, my God!' Annabel blanched. 'I've no idea. I—I can't remember too much about ... about last night. I mean ...' she flushed beneath his lazy eyes, gleaming with amusement.

'You must have a terrible memory,' he said softly.

'Because I can remember every wonderful moment, my love!'

'I didn't mean that ... it's just ...' she faltered as he laughed gently.

'I was only teasing you, Bella. I put it on the bedside table when—when I let loose your glorious hair,' he said thickly, gazing down at his future wife, her long tresses spread about her lovely face.

'You looked spectacularly lovely at the ball last night, but even lovelier lying here like this, my dearest, dearest love.' His voice was husky, his eyes darkening with desire as she wound her arms about his neck, her body responding to the increasing urgency of his caressing fingers.

'No, really, Hugh! We ought to be getting up. You can't ... not now ...' she protested halfheartedly, as he bent to possess her lips in a lingering kiss of aching sweetness.

'You must remember the family motto, my adorable Bella. *Hora e Sempre*, which freely translated, means, "Now and Always!" And that,' he murmured huskily as her ardour leapt to meet his, 'expresses my feelings exactly!'

THE PEACOCK

The peacock that made Annabel think for a moment that she was back in England was undoubtedly the blue peacock, indigenous to southeast Asia and India. This is the species most commonly found in the West, kept semidomesticated in parks and gardens.

The large male peafowl, a member of the pheasant family, is known for his unpleasant personality but famed for his beautiful tail – a sweeping train with elongated coverts (feathers that cover the bases of the large tail quills) tipped with colorful eyelike spots. The peacock can lift and fan his tail at will, a shimmering display of iridescent bronze and blue-green usually put on to impress the peahen – and sometimes a human admirer. Surprisingly, for his tail *is* burdensome, the peacock can fly – but only when he has to!

The national bird of India, the peacock has always been valued there – and not just for his beauty. He destroys cobras; he warns animals when large predatory cats are on the prowl; and he unfailingly predicts, with his harsh cry, when rain is coming.

Probably brought to Europe by ancient Phoenician traders, the peacock plays a role in Greek mythology. According to one famous myth, the ravishing Hera, wife of Zeus, the king of the gods, became jealous when Zeus fell in love with Io. To protect Io from Hera, Zeus changed Io to a heifer. Hera then sent Argus, who had eyes all over his body, to keep watch on the heifer – but Zeus had Argus lulled to sleep and killed. Hera then took Argus's hundred eyes and placed them on the tail of the peacock.

The jealous and shrewish Hera and the notoriously bad-tempered peacock are perhaps a good match. Both are beautiful to look at, but both prove that beauty is only skin deep!

Yours FREE, with a home subscription to SUPEROMANCE™

Complete and mail
the coupon below today!

FREE!

Mail to: SUPEROMANCE

In the U.S.
2504 West Southern Avenue
Tempe, AZ 85282

In Canada
649 Ontario St.
Stratford, Ontario N5A 6W2

YES, please send me FREE and without any obligation, my **SUPEROMANCE** novel, LOVE BEYOND DESIRE. If you do not hear from me after I have examined my FREE book, please send me the 4 new **SUPEROMANCE** books every month as soon as they come off the press. I understand that I will be billed only $2.50 for each book (total $10.00). There are no shipping and handling or any other hidden charges. There is no minimum number of books that I have to purchase. In fact, I may cancel this arrangement at any time. LOVE BEYOND DESIRE is mine to keep as a FREE gift, even if I do not buy any additional books.

NAME _____ (Please Print)

ADDRESS _____ APT. NO. _____

CITY _____

STATE/PROV. _____ ZIP/POSTAL CODE _____

SIGNATURE (If under 18, parent or guardian must sign.)

134 BPS KAK7

SUP-SUB-1

This offer is limited to one order per household and not valid to present subscribers. Prices subject to change without notice. Offer expires September 30, 1984